THE
BROKEN

CONTROL

A. L. FRANCES

Ruby Rose Publishing

Amazon PAPERBACK
© Copyright 2020
A.L Frances

A CIP catalogue record for this title is available from the American/British Library.

ISBN 978-0-9601051-2-0

Amazon is an imprint of Ruby Rose Publishing House.
www.RubyRosePublishingHouse.com

First Published in 2020
Amazon
Printed & Bound in Great Britain

AUTHOR'S NOTE

My purpose for writing the series of *The Broken* novels extends above and beyond just wanting to write a gripping close to home story.

On occasions, I've picked up books and been unable to visualize what the writer has so beautifully written for me. Then, when I've found a book I've loved and read it to the end, the sense of achievement is immeasurable. I believe everyone should embrace this emotion when they read.

My desire is for you to feel just as wonderful when you reach the end of this novel, as I've written this wholeheartedly for you!

DEDICATION

I wrote this for you…

A. L. Frances

CONTENTS

PROLOGUE

The predator and the prey scenario. A cycle of life and death. A cycle that takes place during the fast-paced motion of the day and equally throughout the deathly silence of the night, the strong hunting the weak. Although, it must be noted, no one is untouchable in this world. The predator can also become the prey. This dangerous cycle can change at any given moment and the strong can just as easily become the weak. Let it be known, there isn't a single soul that is safe from the hunt.

We're all susceptible to having our minds corrupted and becoming someone else's target. Other people will own tiny parts of our thoughts throughout our lifetime in one way or another, and the saddest part is that we, as individuals, aren't even aware of it. We believe we have total control over ourselves, we believe we are the masters of our minds, when in fact, we don't see the external response or even recognise the internal split-second rush of anxiety we experience when these influential people arrive in our presence, the superiors so to speak, the ones we each – "answer to". Whether it's a relationship with a spouse, your children or other family member, a barking employer, colleague or part of our ever-growing demanding clientele, the list of individuals who actually have the ability to control and cast some form of influence over our thoughts is endless.

Just think about it for a second: we all have to answer to someone. No matter how stubborn or strong we believe we are, that person owns a section of our mind, and, let's face it, if we can allow them to gain such a substantial amount of power and control over us then what's to stop another from gaining the same?

Think of this: what do you believe your stance in life is? Who do you consider yourself to be? Well, no matter what you consider your status to be, you are, in some way, controlled by another. Remember, there isn't a single mind on this planet that remains untouchable.

We're raised by people older than us and spend years being dictated to. These elders train our minds and program us. We are taught that respect is to obey our superiors. We are consistently told what we can and cannot do – told how we should behave, what language to speak, how to think and even told what foods to like and dislike. We believe this level of order and higher ranking goes away when we hit adulthood. Oh, how wrong are we! This susceptibility to control sits deep within us. So, now you've worked that out as an adult, answer me this: how vulnerable do you feel?

Based on that answer, now try to imagine how vulnerable our young must feel… the untrained minds of children. We've all been there. We were all but young children once. We're all aware of how easy it was during our childhood for someone to come along and lure our minds away. We were innocent, we were vulnerable, we believed what we were told and maybe, just maybe, those elders abused that position and control. The ones who were supposed to protect us… and yet they left us.

Not every child in the world is loved by their biological parents. These same vulnerable children don't have a warm home, or protection from a loved one; they remain wide open to being controlled by another, and it's not always in the right way. These vulnerable young individuals have a voice but are never heard. These are the predator's favourite kind of minds. But once they are controlled, can they be saved? Can the mind be retrained? Can we free the prey? Can we change the cycle?

There is one man who will stop at nothing to free the mind of his daughter, even if this brings him to his death. With more willpower than ever, this determined individual now has help. No longer doubted, no longer labelled a mad man and a murdering scumbag, Matthew Honey has a team ready to assist him with hunting the unknown. But, even with this help, the question remains: since the predator who has full control over his daughter's soul has slipped the net for a second time, where will Matthew begin…?

CHAPTER 1

Ashes to Ashes, Dust to Dust

Positioned in the heart of South Manchester, Southern Cemetery is the final resting place for most of Greater Manchester's dearly departed. Some call it the land of the dead – others, the land of the loved. A home to many and a place of comfort to most.

It's a hot midsummer's morning and the trees are blowing gently as the breeze hits. The grass is a radiant shade of green, and the sky is the brightest of blues. The clouds are few and far between. The grounds of the cemetery are extremely busy, with cars and people crowding the space. The day might be beautiful, but the atmosphere is tense. The people are quiet and still, with tissues in their hands and blotches on their faces. Each attendee is here for the same purpose. They're here to pay their respects and say goodbye to a loved one.

Standing tall and positioned deep into the grounds of the cemetery is one of the four exquisitely constructed chapels. Built with magnificently crafted, stained-glass windows the building is astonishing from the outside and equally as breath-taking on the inside. At centre stage inside, the main focus of the room are two huge, floor length, deep red, velvet curtains which are currently drawn.

Standing by the doorway, the family members of the dearly departed are getting ready for the hardest day of their lives. The final farewell.

"Florence, I'm so sorry for your loss, dear. Dorothy was one of the kindest women I've ever known. Your sister will be missed. As for poor Alice – I have no words. Just know that we are all here for you."

"Thank you, Doris."

Hugging Florence, Doris makes her way into the chapel to lay the bouquet of flowers she has in her hand. Greeting the next person, Florence tries her hardest to remain strong. She never in her life believed she would be attending her younger sister's funeral and most certainly not her niece's.

"Thank you for coming, Stephen."

"Florence, how are you holding up?"

"About as well as can be."

The guests are arriving thick and fast. The sun beams in through the chapel windows, creating a radiant glow and illuminating the space. Unfortunately for those attending today's service, the sun's also radiating an intense amount of heat and the chapel's temperature is becoming somewhat unbearable.

Today's ceremony is somewhat of a rarity: a double cremation. The service is about to start as groups of people of various ages, dressed from head to toe in black, begin walking down the aisle. Taking their seats in silence, the attendees greet each other with nods and sympathetic smiles.

At the front of the chapel stands the widow of one of the deceased, Phil Parkinson. His eyes are bright red and swollen from all the tears he's shed. Phil's struggling to hold it together. He couldn't face standing at the door to greet people. He has no desire to speak to a single person. He just wants to say goodbye to his wife. This broken man has lost not only his soulmate, he has also lost all five of his children. A man who once had it all now has nothing!

Everyone he knows turned their backs on him when they found out that he faked his own death. Alice never cashed in the insurance claims and the investments, so no crime was committed, but what Phil did was way worse. He committed the ultimate sin – he left his family vulnerable to the predators that scavenge amongst us. And in return, he has paid the ultimate price! The loss of it all.

With no one to turn to, Phil has leaned on one particular person for support. An individual he has known for only a matter of weeks, and yet he finds himself bearing his heart and soul to this man.

Sitting at the side of Phil Parkinson, trying his hardest not to freak out and run a million miles, is Matthew Honey. He's fidgeting in his seat; his palms are sweating and he's becoming more and more agitated by the second. Matthew has absolutely no desire to deal with this sad event while sober. Breathing deeply, he's desperately trying to hold it together for Phil, but he's genuinely struggling. This devastating occasion sits too close to his own personal life. The flashbacks are coming thick and fast and are making him feel sick to his stomach. Attempting to distract himself, Matthew begins fiddling with the order of service booklet, avoiding eye contact with anyone.

The time is now ten thirty in the morning on the twenty-seventh of July. As the final few people arrive, two family members close the huge solid-oak doors. Almost immediately, the curtains at the front begin to open.

Positioned on the podium are two solid, dark-oak coffins. The final resting place for mother and daughter. Inside one of the beautifully crafted wooden boxes on pure white cushioned silk is the body of Alice Parkinson. And in the other, the body of her mother, Dorothy Davies.

"Why? Oh God, Alice! Why my Alice?" Phil cries out, with tears streaming down his face and fluid gushing uncontrollably from his nose, "I'm sorry, I'm so fucking sorry, my queen." Looking to Matthew, he screams, "What the fuck, man? What the fuck? What – the – fuck?"

Attempting to be strong, Matthew reaches across to his friend and places his hand on his shoulder. He whispers in his ear, "Phil, I'm here. Come on, you can do this. Be strong for everyone here."

"Fuck it. Be strong? That's my fucking queen in that box. Alice, baby, I'm sorry!"

Seeing that the Reverend has appeared and aware the service is about to start, Matthew attempts to calm Phil down one final time.

"Look around you. All these people are here to pay their respects to Alice and Dorothy. Allow them this." Seeing Phil calm slightly, Matthew continues, "There are children here. They're getting scared. Just hold it together."

At these words, Phil appears to gain some control. Matthew looks over his shoulder, scanning the chapel. There's a sea of people all crying silently. His heart begins to race at a hundred miles per hour. Holding his chest, Matthew breathes deeply and closes his eyes. He's trying not to have a panic attack. Suddenly an image of Alice swinging from a rope flashes at the forefront of his mind. Rapidly opening his eyes, Matthew puts his hand to his mouth to hold in the vomit that has shot up from his stomach.

The reverend takes her place at the front of the chapel. With her shoulders back and her head held high, she begins, "Today's service is one of great sadness. Both mother and daughter are no longer with us in body form, but may I remind each of you that they are present with us in spirit today."

A child shouts from the back, "Mummy, why is Auntie Alice's picture up there?"

"Carlos, shhh, darling, mummy will tell you later."

"But wh…"

"Sweetie, please be quiet, the lady is speaking."

Hearing this innocent child's voice sets a shiver up Matthew's spine. His thoughts go to Phil's five missing children. He hopes the reverend won't mention them.

The reverend clears her throat and continues, "I apologise about that. The family of Alice and Dorothy would like to thank you all for being here today. Now, on your seats you will see that you each have a book which contains the order of service today. Please feel free to collect this now. And might I suggest that since the chapel is somewhat overcrowded today, perhaps you'd be kind enough to share with those next to you and pass some back."

She waits a brief moment for everyone to get settled before proceeding, "The first part of today's service is remembrance. Please, let us bow our heads while we take a moment to remember Alice and Dorothy. Think of those moments that will comfort you in times of

4

need. The memories you shared, the laughter, the joy, the smiles and all the bits in between. Let's take some time to reflect on those special moments. For this part of the service, the family have selected a song for us to listen to as we embrace these dear memories."

As the music starts, Phil places his head in his hands. He's sobbing louder and louder. The song that's playing has deep meaning. It was played during his first dance with his wife at their wedding. Every person in the room has their eyes closed as the tears slowly trickle down their faces.

With his chest getting tighter and tighter, Matthew can't bear it anymore. Looking to the podium he sees sunflowers galore. He sees a picture of his wife and his wife's coffin on the stand. He becomes dizzy and delirious, his head starting to spin. His mind is projecting his wife's funeral, "Lauren…" he whispers.

He looks around the room, but he can barely see what's in front of him. His sight has gone completely hazy. The loss of his vision makes Matthew feel claustrophobic. His hand goes to his throat – he's struggling to breathe. Looking at the masses of bodies all dressed in black, Matthew decides he needs some space and fresh air.

"Mate, you okay…?" Phil asks, turning to face him.

As Phil's voice echoes around his mind, Matthew stands. He slowly manages to stagger his way through the crowd of people and heads towards the exit. He has completely lost all control and feels weak. As he tries to open the door, Matthew collapses. He bangs his head on the way down and vomits on the floor. He lands flat on his back and begins convulsing. The whole room gasps and people rush from all directions to Matthew's aid. But he's out cold. His eyes are closed, and he's locked deep within his mind.

"Hello?" Matthew says. He's surrounded by darkness.

He gets no reply. The only sound he can hear is the echoes of his own voice. And yet, this unfortunate situation feels all too familiar to him. He doesn't like it one bit. Scanning his surroundings, Matthew sees a beam of light appearing in the distance. It gets brighter and brighter, slowly blinding him. Raising his arm to protect his sight, he squints as he tries to make out what's creating this light. He smells a sweet scent. The scent is familiar. Alongside this, Matthew hears a gentle humming. Focusing his attention on the light, he suddenly sees a female figure making her way towards him.

Reaching out his arms, he shouts, "Eve... it's you! Darling, come here to me. I want to save you."

The figure floats closer to him and he sees his daughter is cradling a baby in a blanket. Struggling up onto his feet, Matthew continues, "Eve, is that Hope? Quickly, princess, come to me. I can save you both before she comes back."

"Save her, Dad," Eve shouts, running towards him. She throws the baby in the blanket to him.

"Eve, keep running! I can save you!" Matthew shouts.

As the words leave his mouth, Matthew throws himself forward. He's soaking wet from head to toe. Looking around, he realises he is on a hospital stretcher inside the back of an ambulance. There is a female paramedic in the ambulance with her back to him. Panicking, he starts to pull the wires off his body. Hearing the bleeping, the paramedic turns around.

"Oh, no, no, no, no, no, don't do that. Please, keep that on. You're in a critical condition, Matthew. We need to monitor your vitals. You've just had a severe seizure."

Ignoring her, Matthew replies, "No, I don't, I need a drink. I'm not going anywhere with you."

The driver gets out and comes round to the back of the ambulance, "Matthew, I'm Gary. Calm down, mate. We're trying to help you," he says.

"You can help by letting me out of this fucking ambulance," Matthew snaps, feeling ambushed. Pushing past the two of them, Matthew exits the ambulance and goes in search of Phil.

CHAPTER 2

Protection

"Our Father who art in heaven, hallowed be thy name. Thy kingdom come. Thy will be done on earth as it is in heaven. Give us this day our daily bread, and forgive us our trespasses, as we forgive those who trespass against us, and lead us not into temptation, but deliver us from evil. Our Father who art in heaven, hallowed be thy…"

Sister Elisabeth kneels at the end of her old wooden bed with her hands tightly grasped together, placed just above her head. A candle glows gently in the corner of the room. The small flicker from the candlelight shows her gaunt looking facial features. Her skin complexion is pale and yet she has bright, electric blue, piercing eyes that standout. With her tiny frame, Sister Elisabeth's robes hang heavy on her body. Having taken her vows many years ago, devoting her life to God, Sister Elisabeth has always been considered a faithful, dedicated and precious member of the Moycullen convent. But on this particular evening, she is not considered a loyal member of the convent and has been left to conduct her evening prayer alone. And the prayer she repeats is being submitted with different intentions. She has been ostracized by her fellow sisters for her beliefs and is filled with fear, unsure if the Lord himself is hearing her prayers.

Vulnerable, anxious and feeling isolated, Sister Elisabeth cannot ignore the voices in her head. As the incessant rantings take over,

7

she's being told that something of an impure nature has intruded into their once protected holy establishment. Not only this, the relentless voices are screaming at her that she needs to remove everyone and quickly as the evil force is getting stronger with every second. Sister Elisabeth has tried on multiple occasions to cry for help but has been unsuccessful.

Concerned by her insane rantings, the other sisters had to make an executive decision. Left with no other choice, they have resorted to desperate measures and locked Sister Elisabeth inside her room.

She recites the Lord's Prayer over and over. Feeling more exposed to the dark spirits than ever before, Sister Elisabeth squeezes the rosary beads that hang around her neck for protection.

Suddenly she hears a whisper and the candle blows out. The energy in the room shifts. Desperately trying not to give the whisper any of her attention, Sister Elisabeth squeezes her eyelids together. She doesn't want to see or even acknowledge whatever has entered her room. Fear quickly takes over her thoughts and tears fall one after the other from her eyes. Reciting her prayer over and over, she begs the Lord for protection.

"Our Father who art in heaven, hallowed be thy name. Thy kingdom come. Thy will be done on earth as it is in heaven. Give us this day our daily bread, and forgive us our trespasses, as we forgive those who trespass against us…"

Her senses on high alert, she hears a creak come from the floorboards just inside her doorway. She freezes and stops praying. Reluctantly, she opens her eyes. She's surrounded by the darkness of the night. A chill blows across her face. Sister Elisabeth is no longer alone.

Hidden within the darkest depths of Moycullen Forest in southern Ireland is one of the country's longest standing convents; Moycullen Nunnery. With a medieval theme, this building has retained its fourteenth-century, gothic, architectural design. The grey stone walls are covered with green moss. Positioned at the front of the dark building is an oversized, arched wooden door. A brisk wind is blowing, forcing the round gold knocker to lift and create a repetitive tapping sound. Small, white wooden arched windows are positioned with perfect symmetry throughout the exterior. Each of the windows is weathered and worn. At present, the darkness of the night has fallen and the dim lights inside the convent can be seen flickering through the windows. Mirroring the nunnery's architectural design and positioned directly next to it is the outdoor chapel, which is predominantly used for afternoon prayer and confession. At present the chapel is empty. These eerie-looking buildings are surrounded by fifteen-foot black metal gates and fences. Moycullen Nunnery is home to twenty religious sisters, fifty orphaned children of all different ages and multiple staff members, all of whom are male. The Sisters of Moycullen have their work cut out for them looking after the young, while also fighting against the system to stop the nunnery from being shut down.

The isolated Moycullen Forest is no longer considered to be an appropriate place to raise vulnerable young people, although the Sisters of Moycullen beg to differ and remain united. Their faith and belief in what they have is strong, the sisters have closed the gates to Moycullen Nunnery and continue to protest in order to keep their home.

Inside this secluded establishment, the original fourteenth-century fixtures and fittings are in pristine condition. The hallways are thin, long and lit dimly by small candles fixed at regular distances along the walls.

The rattle of keys echo in the distance. Sister Marie is making her way to the smaller internal chapel for this evening's prayers, her keys swinging from the black woven belt around her oversized waist. Her expression is stern. She has dark brown eyes, with tiny wrinkles around the edges. Age has certainly started to catch up with Sister Marie. On a clear mission, she rushes through the huge solid dark oak doors into the chapel in a fluster and sits down next to Sister Cathleen, joining her fellow sisters for prayer. Sister Cathleen is much younger than Sister Marie, and unlike Sister Marie, she's on the dainty side. Peering across to her fellow sister, Sister Cathleen scrunches her nose and smiles, causing her freckles to gather. Her radiant green eyes beam as she gazes at Sister Marie. Looking around,

Sister Marie then turns to Sister Cathleen and whispers, "Where's Sister Jesselle?"

"I'm not sure," Sister Cathleen whispers back, as she returns to her prayer position.

To the left of Sister Marie sits Sister Alannah. Glowing, beautiful, Sister Alannah. She has hazel eyes, natural thick lashes and a nose that slopes to perfection with a tiny little point. Peering to her left, Sister Marie whispers, "Sister Alannah, have you seen Sister Jesselle anywhere?"

This sister doesn't move her head, "No, last I heard she was conducting this evening's prayer with the children, in their room," she says.

"Why? What's the rush?" asks Sister Cathleen, looking up at Sister Marie once more.

"Sister Elisabeth is howling in her room again. It's echoing down the halls. Except this time she's screaming a name and it sounds like Jesselle."

Now too peering up, Sister Alannah says, "What do you think?"

"Sisters, I don't know, but in all my thirty years at the convent, I've never heard screams like it. It sent chills through my bones and made my hairs stand to attention."

"What do you think we should do?" Sister Alannah says with a look of concern fast spreading across her face.

"After prayer, we will go and check," Sister Marie says, also looking concerned. "But for now, sisters, let us pray for her."

Bowing their heads, they anxiously pray in silence for their fellow sister.

Sister Marie leads the way along the hallway with a candle in her hand, Sisters Alannah and Cathleen are trailing slightly behind her. With her commitment and longstanding service to the convent, Sister Marie is now a superior member at Moycullen Nunnery. One of her responsibilities is to hold all the keys for the entire nunnery. Sister Alannah and Sister Cathleen, on the other hand, are not superior. The pair do as they're asked when they're asked and remain in line at all times.

"Sister Marie, are you sure we should be doing this?" Sister Alannah asks nervously. "You know Sister Elisabeth has been confined behind her door for her own safety."

Sister Marie doesn't respond as she continues to march her way down the hallway.

"Sister, please stop and think about this," Sister Alannah pleads.

Sister Marie stops and rolls her eyes.

"What if she overpowers us and escapes?"

"You're being far too suspicious," Sister Marie says in a dismissive tone as she turns to walk away.

Reaching out, Sister Alannah continues, "Sister, you and I both know that if Sister Elisabeth continues with her insane rantings and somehow leaves the nunnery and exposes such things, it will give the officials all the power they need. Each of us will be dragged out one by one and Moycullen will be forced to close its gates forever. We are hanging on by a thread as it is. I do not want to be getting in trouble with Sister Kathryn if Sister Elisabeth escapes. Do you not agree?" She waits a brief moment, but with no response again, Sister Alannah pleads one final time, "We really can't bring attention to the home right now. Sisters, please, I honestly think we should turn back. I don't like the—"

"Shh!" Sister Marie says, putting her finger to her lips. "Sisters, did you hear that?"

"What?" says Sister Cathleen.

"Listen, you can hear the cries of a soul."

"Oh Sister Marie, certainly your imagination must be getting the best of you." Sister Cathleen replies.

"I'm being serious. I can hear her. It's Sister Elisabeth." Standing still, Sister Marie continues, "I fear we're too late."

"Too late for what?" Sister Cathleen asks.

Looking panicked, Sister Alannah turns and attempts to run back to the chapel inside the nunnery, from where they came.

Grabbing her by the arm, Sister Marie says, "No, Sister, we are all in this. You have to see this through."

"Please, Sister, let go of me. I just want to go back. I feel something sinister in the corridors."

"Stop! You must be brave, Sister Alannah. We have the Lord on our side. He will protect us. Please, do not run and I will let go. Remember, we are doing this for our Sister. She needs us right now. Do not think of yourself. Be strong for her."

Hanging her head with defeat, Sister Alannah replies, "Okay, Sister. You are right. Just please let go, you're hurting me."

Sister Marie is desperate to get to Sister Elisabeth, but she doesn't want to do it alone. In a bid to keep her two sisters with her, she says, "Both of you, please remember why we are here right now. We are here for Sister Elisabeth. If I am wrong and she is okay, which I pray I am, then we must let her know that we are here for her. We are the fortunate ones. Can you imagine all your sisters turning against you? She must feel extremely vulnerable right now. If the evil she speaks of has in fact intruded within our walls, then she is the weakest of us all. As we know, sisters, evil feeds from fear. We can only trust that our Lord is protecting her from any malevolent spirits."

They continue on their way towards Sister Elisabeth's room, each of them praying for protection.

Her apprehension building, Sister Marie can feel the energy of something impure circulating around them. Slowly taking one step at a time, she breathes deeply. The further down the corridor she gets, the more nervous she becomes. The candle in her hand begins to flicker. She sees this but she can't feel any breeze, and fear takes over her mind.

Sister Alannah squeezes her rosary beads tightly and Sister Cathleen firmly holds her cross. They begin quietly reciting The Lord's Prayer.

"Our Father who art in heaven, hallowed be thy name. Thy kingdom come. Thy will be done on earth as it is in heaven. Give us this day our daily bread, and forgive us our trespasses, as we forgive those who trespass against us, and lead us not into temptation, but deliver us from evil."

They arrive at Sister Elisabeth's room. Not a sound can be heard. Tapping on the door, Sister Marie says, "Sister Elisabeth, are you in there?"

There's no reply.

Tapping once more, she says, "Sister Elisabeth, is everything okay?"

Still no response.

Turning to the others, Sister Marie says, "What shall we do?"

"Do you have the master key, Sister?" Sister Cathleen asks.

Sister Marie says, "Yes." And with her hands shaking slightly, she riffles through the mound of keys she has on the metal loop hanging from her waist. Eventually finding the master key, she holds it in her hand and breathes deeply as she unlocks the door.

The door creaks as it opens slightly. There is a strong stench and the sisters all cover their noses. A gust of wind blows out the candle. Peering in the room, Sister Marie sees a tiny glow at the back wall. She pushes the door completely open. With a huge sigh of relief, she sees Sister Elisabeth. She's got her back to the door and is sitting up right at her desk.

"Sister Elisabeth?" Sister Marie whispers nervously.

She gets no reply.

She walks slowly into the room.

"Sister Elisabeth, are you okay? I heard screams coming from your room and we thought we would come and check on you."

There is still no reply and not so much as a flinch from Sister Elisabeth.

Sister Cathleen and Sister Alannah move inside the room and join Sister Marie. Slowly placing one foot in front of the other, Sister Marie inches towards Sister Elisabeth. Tears are forming in her eyes and she is praying under her breath. She reaches out and places her hand on Sister Elisabeth's shoulder.

Sister Elisabeth turns her head and stares at Sister Marie's hand, then suddenly jumps up from her seat. Her eyes are like gaping holes in her face. She screams out at her sisters, her teeth bared.

The three sisters all turn and run towards the door. Sister Alannah doesn't even look back and keeps on running towards the chapel. Stopping at the door, Sister Marie puts out her arm so that Sister Cathleen doesn't leave her alone.

"We've come this far," Sister Marie says.

They both reluctantly turn around. Sister Elisabeth is standing at the desk in her room, staring at them blankly, her head slightly tilted to one side. Drool travels down her chin and she appears to be humming under her breath.

Making her way back into the room, Sister Marie says, "Sister Elisabeth, can you hear me?"

"Go away," Sister Elisabeth replies.

"Sister Elisabeth, we're worried about you. I heard screams."

Sister Elisabeth's face remains motionless as she replies, "You heard nothing, I am fine. Now leave!"

Scared but not wanting to leave her alone, Sister Marie slowly makes her way closer to Sister Elisabeth, "I just want to make sure you are okay."

Sister Elisabeth growls and reveals her teeth, "I said leave!" she shouts, her voice abnormally deep.

"Come on, Sister," Sister Cathleen says, grabbing Sister Marie's arm. "We have seen her now, she is okay. Let us leave her be." Turning to Sister Elisabeth she says, "Sister Elisabeth, we are sorry to have intruded on you. We will leave you for the evening."

Sister Marie is unconvinced, but she gives in. "Okay, we will leave as you wish, Sister. I will come back tomorrow."

"I suggest you do not return to my room or you will pay the price."

"What? Pay the price..." says Sister Marie, startled by her words. "Sister Elisabeth, what has gotten into you? I fear for you being left here alone."

"I am not alone. Now you should listen to your sister beside you and leave."

"She is your sister, too."

Sister Elisabeth's facial expression turns dark, "I said leave!" she shouts.

Sister Cathleen drags Sister Marie out of the room and slams the door shut. Not giving up, Sister Marie calls through the door, "Sister Elisabeth, the children are asking for you. Please, if you need any of us, we are here, we have not left you. I will never give up on you, you're my sister."

14

"I will never leave the children and I have no sisters," Sister Elisabeth shouts back.

Sister Elisabeth sits back down at her desk. The candle flickers away. Her back is completely straight and she's staring at nothing, her features motionless. Suddenly, her eyes change. Every molecule is taken over as they turn jet-black. Not a patch of white can be seen.

Embracing the pain she's feeling, Sister Elisabeth chants, "Thy will be done on earth as it is in hell." A sudden gust of wind blows out the candle. "You were right," Sister Elisabeth says. "I serve you. I will assist you. I accept my fate."

No sooner has Sister Elisabeth made this statement and accepted her fate, the candle reignites.

Standing behind her is her new owner. It's Jezebel. Leaning to her ear, Jezebel whispers, "Your soul is mine."

As soon as the words leave her lips, Sister Elisabeth begins to transform into a mirror image of the evil entity standing behind her. Her skin turns grey and deep black cracks appear upon her skin, oozing a thick black substance.

Jezebel makes her way around the desk. She gazes at Sister Elisabeth through the gap in her long black hair. The thick black substance gushes from her mouth as she says, "Put your arms on the table."

Instantly reacting to this command, Sister Elisabeth puts her arms onto the table.

"Turn your hands over."

Again, Sister Elisabeth does as she's told. Reaching across, Jezebel reveals Sister Elisabeth's wrists. Digging her razor-sharp nail into Sister Elisabeth's skin, she penetrates the surface and engraves an upside-down cross on her flesh. Collecting the black substance from around her mouth, Jezebel presses this into the wounds she's she has just created.

Sister Elisabeth remains completely still. Her soul is no longer her own and she is now a possession of the evil that has intruded into this once protected home. With a blank expression upon her face, Sister Elisabeth says, "I will serve you."

"You will serve your purpose and nothing more," Jezebel intones. "You have been chosen purely because of your role. The sister who has the closest bond with all of the children. That sister, is you." Holding Sister Elisabeth by the chin, Jezebel stares directly in her eyes and continues, "A victim all those years ago when you were but a child. Taunted by your recent nightmares. Slowly losing your faith bit by bit. I promise you this: I will relieve you of your pain. But, should you betray me, you will die."

The candle suddenly goes out. Within a second, flames light up all around the room. Standing in the centre in their true demonic forms are Eve, Lewis, Freddie, Rupert, Terence and Jezebel, who is cradling baby Hope.

Getting up from her chair, Sister Elisabeth makes her way to her new owners. Bowing and falling to her knees, she says, "I am here to serve you all. I will never betray you, Dark Empress."

CHAPTER 3

Where Are They?

I t's now March. The months have passed since Phil said his final farewell to his wife Alice and mother-in-law Dorothy. Struggling every day to come to terms with the loss of his family and disgraced by his actions, Phil has not been taking care of himself. Giving up all hope, he has attempted suicide four times. Fortunately for Phil, Matthew has been his saviour. Advised by his doctor that he was going to be sectioned for his own safety if he continued to harm himself, Phil decided to accept Matthew's offer and has now taken refuge at Matthew's home, which has now been restored to its previous organised state.

At present, it's mid-afternoon and Phil is in the day room. He can see the tide is out. Golden sand travels for miles and the bright blue sea is resting in the distance. Phil is gently pushing his feet on the floor, slowing moving back and forth on the rocking chair by the window. Distracted for a brief moment, he's locked into a daze as he's gazing at the tranquillity of the beach during the natural daylight. Phil sits in silence, breathing deeply. His eyes suddenly well up. Swallowing the lump that has developed at the back of his throat, Phil closes his eyes as a single tear begins rolling down his cheek. Phil wipes it and glances at the thick, once cream-colored and now grimy bandage wrapped tightly around his wrist. With a deep sigh, he hangs his head in shame. Looking to the table positioned next to him, Phil retrieves the whiskey glass and throws the remainder of the contents to the back of his throat. Scrunching up his face, Phil scowls as the whiskey burns its way down and warms his stomach. Hearing the creaking of the floorboards, Phil peers across to the doorway. He sees Matthew enter with a concerned smile on his face.

"Please, don't say anything," Phil says as he looks at the empty whiskey glass in his hand and turns back to face the window.

"I wasn't going to say anything negative to you," Matthew responds as he makes his way into the room and seats himself on the sofa facing Phil.

"Good," Phil replies sternly.

"Are you hungry? I've made some fresh pasta for lunch."

"Thanks, but I don't feel like eating right now."

"Okay, that's fine."

The pair sit in silence for a brief moment.

Breathing deeply once again, still staring out of the window, Phil says, "How do you do it?"

"Do what?"

"How do you stay so strong and continue to live?"

"Believe me, Phil, I was never this strong. I was once where you are now. Drinking myself to oblivion. I desperately wanted to get Eve back but at the same time I was wishing for death so that I didn't have to feel the pain in my heart anymore. But Phil, the only thing the alcohol gave me was an extra illness and an extra battle. Alongside the mental torture of wanting to get Eve back, I also had to deal with my addiction to alcohol and the physical pain that came along with it. It was what made me weak and not want to live anymore."

Phil hangs his head as he begins processing the words Matthew has just said. Deep down he knows Matthew is right. Every day his body is getting weaker, he's becoming a victim to the addiction. Shaking, vomiting, constant headaches, pain in his right side, taunting thoughts, the list is endless. And then when he finally has a drink, like a cure, the pain suddenly goes away and the taunting voices in his head stop. He isn't stupid, he knows his drinking is a problem and it will never help him get what he truly wants – his children back. His voice low, Phil replies to Matthew's concerns, "I know what you are saying, Matthew. I just don't know how to get out of it."

"It's okay. You don't have to know the answers. Believe me, I've been where you are. I've walked in your shoes. You can get better. Look at me, I have. I'm living proof that this will not last forever. I know more than anyone what you're going through, Phil. Why do you think I offered up my home to you?"

This time Phil doesn't answer the question.

"I did this selflessly because I wanted to help you get better so that we can get our children back. The twelfth step in recovery states that it is my duty as an alcoholic in recovery to carry the message to other alcoholics and practise the principles in all our affairs. By this, it's my duty to help others who are struggling with the same illness." Matthew leans forward to Phil and looks him directly in the eye. "Phil, I've been sober for almost eight months now. The last drink I had was the night before Eve got taken from me again. From that moment on, I realized that if I hadn't wasted so much time drowning my sorrows there's a chance that I might have found her sooner and I would have possibly gotten her back. My drinking slowed me down. Phil, I don't want the same for you. Wasted time is no good to anyone, especially your missing children."

Wiping his face once more, Phil says, "You're right, there's no doubt in my mind about it. But Matthew, I just don't want to deal with the pain of withdrawal right now."

"Why not? There's no time like the present."

Phil again doesn't respond, he's feeling anxious about the possibility of going through the pain of withdrawal and detoxing his body.

"You're not alone now, Phil. You have me. A fellow addict in active recovery. We can work the twelve steps together. I can help you, Phil, but only if you want the help." There's a brief moment of silence. Matthew then continues, "Eve has been gone for twenty months now. Honestly, it doesn't get any easier. The pain, the loss, the gaping hole in my life, it will not be filled until I have her here where she belongs. But for now, I have to hold on to my faith, and believe that my search and commitment to bring her home will be rewarded."

Phil's hands begin to tremble. His internal voice starts to taunt him. In a panic, Phil bellows, "I can't, I'm not as strong as you. I can't do it."

Making his way to the rocking chair, Matthew kneels at the side of a teary-eyed Phil, "You can do this. But like I've said, you have to want to. Promise me you will think about it."

Crying, Phil says, "Where are they, Matthew? They've been missing for eight months now. Where are my babies?" Phil breaks down.

Matthew holds Phil, "We will find them. Have faith, my friend, I promise. Phil, I just need you to get better, you're no good to them in this state."

"I'm scared," Phil whispers.

"I've got you. Don't be scared."

Looking at Matthew, Phil sees his smile. Feeling relived that he has such a strong individual by his side, who has already walked in his shoes, Phil takes in a deep breath and smiles back. Suddenly, Matthew's phone begins to ring. Taking the phone from out of his pocket, Matthew answers the call. He then stands and leaves the room. Composing himself, Phil wipes his eyes, "Come on, Phil, you can do this. You can get through this." Giving himself a pep talk he continues, "Matthew's right, the kids need me and they need me to get better and be strong for them." Looking up at the sky he says, "Queen, I won't let you down anymore."

Around five minutes pass and Matthew enters the day room looking confused as he seats himself back onto the sofa.

"Who was it?" Phil says.

"Erm, it was DCS Terry."

"Really, what did he want? We haven't heard from him for ages."

"He said Lamont is up for dismissal and he's likely gonna get the boot from the force any day now."

"What?" Phil says as he sits bolt upright in his seat.

"Yeah. He also said that he's been thinking and he wants to help me try and get Eve back."

"Wait, I'm so confused, why now?"

"He's said that he's had enough. So many of his colleague's lives have been ruined because of Jezebel and he now wants to get justice for them."

"Do you believe him?"

"Yeah, he seemed pretty genuine, to be honest. He also said he wants a meeting with me at Headquarters down at Scotland Yard on Saturday fifteenth."

"Wait, that's just two days away. What did you say?"

"Well, I said yes of course and told him you'd be coming too."

"Me, really?"

"Yeah, your kids have been taken as well. We're part of this together now." Scratching his head, Matthew appears stunned.

Blown away himself, Phil replies, "Okay. Well, I suppose there's no harm in seeing what he has to say."

"That's the spirit, mate," Matthew says with a smile on his face. "You ready to conquer your illness and get better?"

"Yeah, I am," Phil responds with a brave and eager smile.

"Right, that's that, then. Now, come on, let's get you some food," Matthew says.

"Okay," Phil replies as he stands.

CHAPTER 4

Hello Honey

"**S**ister Jesselle, let us in. She is in pain." Sister Kathryn pleads.

"Sisters, your assistance is not needed," Sister Jesselle says, guarding the door.

Sister Jesselle pushes Sister Kathryn away from the room. She is on the short side but with a stocky frame. Sister Kathryn stumbles back, knocking into Sister Jennifer, who is standing directly behind her. Sister Jennifer, who is taller than Sister Kathryn but on the thin side, is struck with enough force to send her reeling and tripping over her own feet until she lands on the floor. Panicking, Sister Kathryn quickly bends down and retrieves a slightly red-faced Sister Jennifer from off the ground. "My goodness, are you okay, Sister?"

"I'm fine," Sister Jennifer responds as she begins dusting herself off.

Amused by her bullying antics, Sister Jesselle, with her head held high, proudly says, "I am the superior Sister of this establishment. Now do as I say and go back about your business."

"Watch your tongue, Sister," snaps Sister Kathryn, who has been a Sister of Moycullen for over thirty years. "In actual fact, I am the Mother Superior of this convent and here we pride ourselves on our united sisterhood, we all serve one another with the same level of respect. Your higher ranking is in your own head; you do not have ownership of us. We are the sisters of Moycullen and have been for many years. You might have been a Superior Sister at your previous convent, but your mere eight months here have not earned you such a title."

Smirking, Sister Jesselle slowly makes her way towards Sister Kathryn. Standing her ground, Sister Kathryn also has her head held high. An agonising scream is heard from inside the room. Sister Jesselle's smirk grows as she says, "Luck is on your side this time, Sister."

Sister Jesselle disappears inside the room and the door locks.

"Sister, let's leave," Sister Kathryn says. "We will have to pray for our resident's safe arrival."

Following her down the corridor, Sister Jennifer says nothing.

Behind the locked door, the room is gloomy, lit only by candlelight. Eve lies in bed with a wet towel pressed against her head. It's the fourteenth of March and she's now thirty-five weeks pregnant and her waters have broken, forcing her into early labour. Standing at the side of the bed and holding her hand is Lewis.

"You can do this, baby girl," he says, as he kisses her on the head.

She bellows with pain.

"It's all going to be over with soon. I promise," Lewis reassures her.

Eve doesn't want to hear his words of encouragement. He has no clue what she's going through, "Lewis, I can't do this," she shouts.

Sister Jesselle makes her way to the bedside and moves Lewis aside. Stroking Eve's hair, she says, "Eve, you must. This is part of your fate."

Wanting the whole thing to be over, Eve closes her eyes and pushes with all her might. Young, scared and with no one to guide her, unfortunately, she has pushed too soon. She feels a pop and a surging pain as her insides rip. Eve screams. Almost instantly, the bedsheets she's lying on turn red. Dizzy and feeling as if at any moment she's about to throw up, Eve looks to Lewis. Her sight has gone hazy and both Lewis and Sister Jesselle are slowly fading away.

With one last blink, the room turns pitch black. Drifting in and out of consciousness, Eve whispers, "Help me…" No sooner has she murmured the words, Eve's out cold!

Standing in complete darkness, Eve looks down. She's surprised to see that she's cradling what appears to be a baby inside a white sheet. Gently bouncing the baby up and down she says, "Oh my goodness, baby, baby, baby, it's going to be okay, I'm here." Looking around, she sees nothing but a blanket of darkness. Becoming fearful of her surroundings, Eve says, "Hello… Lewis…? Jess…?"

There is nothing but deathly silence. This situation feels all too familiar and she doesn't like it. Eve stands perfectly still, trying to process what's happening and why. Confused, she whispers under her breath, "Am I dead?"

Feeling the baby squirm, she decides to look inside the white sheet. Opening it, she sees the baby's naked body. Eve gasps. It's a little girl. With one big silent yawn, the baby girl opens her eyes. Instantly, Eve's heart warms. Looking the sleepy little girl in the eye and not wanting to startle her, Eve whispers, "Are you mine?"

A rush of happiness and love surges around her body. Holding this precious little girl is generating feelings she never believed would be possible for her. Wrapped in the moment, Eve doesn't want to take her eyes off this unnamed baby girl. Her tiny fingers rest gently against her face and she's making quiet baby sounds. She's extremely pretty and has the rosiest cheeks. Purity and innocence are locked deep within her eyes – she's perfect, untainted.

Covering the baby's body back up with the white sheet, Eve kisses her gently on the head and cradles her tightly. As she holds the baby girl up against her chest, Eve can't help herself, she begins smelling her brand-new baby smell. With her eyes closed Eve whispers in the baby's ear, "I will love you with all my heart forever. I will look after you, I promise. I will protect you. You are my priority and come first always."

Looking around once more, Eve desperately tries to work out where she is. She hears a loud bang and her heart starts racing. Turning to where the noise came from, Eve sees a spotlight in the distance.

Ensuring she's got a tight grip of the baby, she bravely makes her way towards the light. With each step, her heart pulsates faster and faster. With each pump getting stronger and stronger, Eve feels as if at any given moment her heart's going to burst out of her chest.

Suddenly a deep voice echoes in the distance. Standing stiff, as the voice begins registering inside her mind, Eve can't help but feel a sense of familiarity. She's heard this voice somewhere before, but she can't quite grasp whose it is. The tone is way too deep to be Lewis and the accent is different.

Deciding there's only one way she's going to find out, Eve starts walking towards the light again, picking up her pace. She's nervous and is constantly checking over her shoulder. She feels as though someone is chasing her. But as soon as she turns to check, she sees there's no one there. With all her senses on high alert, Eve jumps when the male voice suddenly shouts, "Eve… it's you! Darling, come here to me. I want to save you."

Eve stops abruptly in her tracks. As she processes the words he has spoken, Eve's heart warms. Something is telling her she knows who this man is. Her heart is aware of who this voice belongs to. With a feeling of love surging through her body, Eve's now more desperate than ever to figure out who this man is. She has a huge urge to run to him but she doesn't know why.

Eve sets off marching closer to the light. She has almost made it. Desperately trying to catch her breath and looking dead ahead, Eve suddenly sees a face appear in the light. Startled by this image, she's now even more puzzled than before. Eve one hundred percent recognises this man.

Following her gut instinct, she runs towards the male figure, the baby held tight in her arms. Eve's getting closer. She's going to make it. She's using all her power to run as fast as she possibly can, and her legs begin to feel heavy. A pain surges down through her muscles. Stumbling to her knees, Eve cries. She holds onto the baby tighter than ever, determined not to give up. Just as she is about to stand, a bone tingling chill tremors all the way down her spine.

Slowly turning, Eve sees Jezebel standing in the background. She's staring at Eve through the gap in her hair. No sooner has Eve made eye contact than she hears the male's voice again, "Quickly, princess, come to me. I can save you both before she comes back."

Eve turns back towards the light, her heart racing faster. She has broken through the mental barrier and worked out who the man is. Tears form in her eyes. She now knows that this is a trap, that she won't make it to him, but that isn't going to stop her from trying. Looking over her shoulder, Eve once again sees Jezebel, except this time, Jezebel is running directly towards her. Making a rash decision, Eve jumps up off the ground and throws the baby towards the light. Distraught, she screams, "Save her, Dad!"

Eve launches herself forward… and finds herself back in bed, soaking wet from head to toe in sweat. Looking down, she sees that the white sheets are drenched with blood. Alone and delirious, Eve's unaware of what has happened to her. With her body at its weakest, she's struggling to move and is in agony. Every part of her body aches and hurts. She gently places her hand on her stomach. As her fingers graze her skin, a huge bolt of pain surges throughout her body. Realising that her baby bump is gone, she begins to panic. Her vagina feels swollen and sore. Frightened, Eve scans the room. There's no Lewis, no Sister Jesselle and no baby.

"Where's my baby?" Eve shouts.

She attempts to get out of the bed, only to slump weakly to the floor. She looks up to see Lewis bursting into the room. He carefully picks her up and places her back inside the bed. Lewis strokes Eve's hair and whispers, "Shhhh, you need to get some rest. I'll go get you some clean sheets."

"No, don't leave me, Lewis. I'm scared."

"Scared…? What of?"

The door is still open and Eve looks up to see Sister Elisabeth in the doorway. She's standing up straight with her shoulders back, staring directly at Lewis and Eve. Her expression is blank, her face is pale white and gaunt, her eyes have dark rims around them and her lips tinged with black. Sister Elisabeth slowly tilts her head to one side. In an emotionless tone she says, "Tell Sister Jesselle I will collect the baby later." She then turns and makes her way back down the hallway.

Mortified by the words Sister Elisabeth has just spoken, Eve looks to Lewis and says, "No she will not. Where's our baby, Lewis?"

"Sshh… don't worry, everything's okay. She's with Sister Jesselle. You lost a lot of blood and we had to pull the baby out of you."

"What do you mean pull the baby out of me? Is it dead?"

Smiling Lewis replies, "No, she's perfectly fine."

"That's twice you've said she…?"

"Yes, we have a healthy baby girl."

"We have a baby girl?"

"Yes. And I just want to say thank you. She's so beautiful."

With tears welling in her eyes Eve says, "I want to see her. Go and collect her from Jess."

"Okay, but you have to promise me you won't try and get out of the bed."

"I promise. Now Lewis, please, go and get my daughter."

Lewis makes his way out of the room, closing the door behind him. Eve waits for what feels like an eternity, getting more and more anxious by the second. All she wants is to hold her baby girl. The baby girl she has felt kicking inside her since she was fifteen weeks pregnant. The baby girl she has fallen in love with while protecting her with her body. And yet now, she's more nervous than ever. Just like that, she's unable to protect this same baby girl. Just like that, she's been ripped from her body. And just like that, she's no longer in control.

As the door handle turns, Eve slowly pulls herself up right. Lewis enters the room and he's empty handed. Panicking, Eve shouts, "Lewis, where is she?"

He sits on the bed and grabs Eve's hands. Smiling he looks her in the eyes and says, "She's…"

But he doesn't have chance to finish, because just then Sister Jesselle enters the room. Held tightly inside her arms is Eve and Lewis's brand-new baby girl, wrapped in a pure white sheet. Reaching out her arms, Eve anxiously says, "Jess, give her to me."

Sister Jesselle walks over to the side of the bed, "Why must you try to disobey me?" she says.

"What are you talking about? Please, Jess, pass her to me."

As she stares down at the baby in the white sheet, suddenly Sister Jesselle's skin tone changes to grey and her eyes turn blood red. Her inner evil is surfacing. Looking at the baby she begins humming. The humming slowly turns to singing.

"Ring a' Ring o' Roses…"

"No! Please don't," Eve screams, hysterical. "I'll do anything. Please don't do this to my baby."

Jezebel locks eyes with Eve, gaining full control over her mind.

"Your soul is mine," she says. "I have told you to stop calling me Jess. It's Sister Jesselle and you'd be wise to remember that. If you continue to disobey me, I will crush your soul and replace it with your child's. Do you understand?"

Eve's eyes have now turned black. A single black tear slowly trickles down her face, as she responds blankly, "Yes."

"Yes, what?"

"Yes, Sister Jesselle."

Lewis stands motionless, his expression blank. He knows who his owner is. He knows who reigns supreme over his existence and so he says nothing. He truly fears the entity who owns his soul.

Returning to her human form, Sister Jesselle leans over to Eve with the baby still in her arms, "You would be wise to keep in mind that you are, and always have been, a possession of mine. You have my DNA surging throughout your veins. You belong to the dark side." Placing her hand under Eve's chin and raising her face, she continues, "We are so close to building our empire and reigning supreme across the universe. Do not allow your human nature to get you killed. Do not sacrifice our destiny. Do not lose sight of the fate that is aligned. Soon enough it will be our time to rule."

Staring in a trance at Sister Jesselle, Eve says nothing.

Placing the baby inside Eve's arms, Sister Jesselle whispers, "Don't get too attached, she's not yours to keep."

Shaking, Eve holds this precious baby girl tightly in her arms. Mentally broken, she begins sobbing. All Eve wants to do is love this baby girl, but now she's too scared to. Bringing the baby up to her face, Eve closes her eyes and kisses her on her forehead. Eve's tears land on her baby's head. Placing her nose onto her daughter's little nose, she feels her warmth and smiles, "Hello, Honey," she whispers.

Lewis comes over and sits next to Eve on the bed, "Honey?" he says.

"Yes, Honey Parkinson."

Sister Jesselle watches the movements of the two new parents from the doorway. Content, she slowly begins transforming into her true demonic form. The transition complete, she stands with her head held low, peering through the gap in her hair. She's aware she has full control. Jezebel is ready to take over the Moycullen Nunnery and will stop at nothing to get her way. This self-sustaining evil entity is about to become unstoppable!

CHAPTER 5

The Smirk

"Bullshit! I built that operation, and you know it!" Chief Inspector Lamont yells, banging his fists on the table in a rage.

He is positioned centre stage at his final misconduct hearing. His fate within the Police Force depends solely on the outcome of this trial. Dressed in his navy-blue suit with his crisp white shirt and deep ruby red silk tie, Lamont looks nothing other than professional. His behaviour, on the other hand, is extremely childlike. He can't help but feel betrayed and ambushed by his colleagues.

He's furious as he has been under review for the past several months and placed on restricted duties. As if that wasn't a big enough blow, he has also been removed from Operation Bee Sting. He was told in a meeting that his superiors felt as though they didn't have a choice – and that they had to take drastic action. Lamont was shocked to hear that complaints had surfaced throughout his career, and they were no longer able to ignore the accusations and assaults to his character and work ethic. As a further insult, one of the members of the meeting suggested to him that he had seen this pattern develop in employees before. A pattern whereby individuals are given power over other people's lives, and sometimes, just sometimes, some members of the Force develop an ugly, godlike mindset. They become solely focused on one mission due to a personal dislike of the individual under investigation. This personal vendetta, in his opinion, makes them lose everything, including their professionalism. Unfortunately for Lamont, Matthew Honey was his personal vendetta. And what's even more unfortunate for him is that Matthew Honey's innocence has been proven and now his unprofessional behaviour has surfaced, raising alarm bells with his superiors.

Firmly stating that they believed Lamont had become blinded by hate and obsessed with placing Matthew Honey behind bars, his superiors have said that instead of actually gathering evidence to find out the truth about what happened to Lauren and Evelyn Jade Honey he neglected the case and only spent time trying to frame Matthew Honey for crimes he did not commit. Now, Lamont's longstanding career, which he has invested his whole life in, is on the line. After all his years of commitment and service to the Force, Lamont has decided they can challenge him all they like, because he's not going down without a fight. Allowing all the pent-up anger and rage that has been building inside of him to take over his mind, Lamont sweeps the stack of paperwork off the desk in front of him and stands from his chair.

Sat in the seat next to Lamont is his lawyer, Alan Rochdale. Shaking his head, he looks across the room at the panel and says, "On behalf of my client, I'd like to apologise." He gets up and continues, "If you would please excuse us for a moment, I'd like to have a private word with my client outside."

Sitting across the way and also shaking her head is Angela Thea, the representative from the Police Federation. Angela's job is to ensure that Lamont has adequate funding and fair legal representation and as today is the final hearing, she has decided to attend in person, "Sure, Mr Rochdale, go ahead," she says.

Alan looks at Lamont and frowns as he says, "Step outside, please."

Rolling his eyes, Lamont reluctantly follows Alan out of the room, slamming the door shut behind him.

Standing in the corridor speaking with Alan, Lamont suddenly feels someone grab his shoulder and pull him back, "What the fuck do you think you're playing at?" Angela barks. Before he has time to answer she says, "Acting like a child – really? Is this what we're doing now?" Again, without giving him time to respond, she continues, "That's it, you can kiss your time on the Force goodbye. God damn it, what is wrong with you?"

Lamont is shocked by her rant. He's also slightly disappointed with himself, as he promised he wouldn't lose his cool. His mouth gaping open, Alan is overseeing the heated discussion between the pair. Noticing the shock on Alan's face, Lamont says, "Alan, can you give us a minute, please?"

Still appearing shocked, he replies, "Erm, of course. I'll go grab a coffee."

"Perfect, thank you."

Grabbing Angela by the arm, Lamont finds the nearest empty room and drags her into it. Locking the door behind him he turns and holds Angela by the face and begins kissing her passionately. Immediately, her body surrenders to his touch. Tugging at her hair slightly, he growls into her ear, "You looked so hot then when you were mad. You have no idea how much I want to fuck you right now."

Angela replies, "Right now?"

"Yes, now."

"But…"

"No buts, I want to be inside you now."

Putting his hands inside her jacket he slowly glides the sleeves down her arms and throws it on the floor. Kissing her again, he unbuttons her shirt, revealing her lace bra, which holds her perfectly perky breasts. His eyes light up. He kisses each of them, loving the feel of her soft skin against his lips. Looking up he sees the pleasure on Angela's face and it makes his erection grow even harder. He makes his way down her toned body and begins tugging on her skirt, revealing her thong. He kisses his way down her lower abdomen. Pulling off her underwear, he puts his head between her legs. She's already extremely wet and he's loving the taste of her.

He can hear her moaning and trying to be quiet as she covers her mouth with her hand. This just turns him on even more. Lamont can see Angela is locked deep within the moment. A huge sense of euphoria surges around his body. Angela grabs his hair and begins rocking his head back and forth as he's burying his tongue deep inside of her. Angela moans out loud, "I want your dick inside me now."

Removing his tongue from her wet vagina, Lamont surfaces. In a low and seductive tone he replies, "Really? How bad do you want me to fuck you right now?'

"Don't play around, put your dick in me."

"Who's playing? I want you to tell me how bad you want me inside you."

"Listen, if you don't put that dick inside me now, I'm going to take what's mine."

Smirking, he replies, "Oh, really? It's like that, is it?"

"Yes."

"Well, I best give you what's yours then, hadn't I…"

Grabbing her by the head and passionately kissing her, Lamont slowly guides her towards the desk in the corner of the room.

Feeling horny and ready to fuck like a porn star, Lamont feels Angela's hand on his trousers, as she's caressing every single inch of him. Lamont is turned on to the maximum, he's loving that Angela is tasting her vagina on his lips and appears to be enjoying it. Reaching the desk, he guides her back and begins undoing his trousers.

"So you want this dick then, do you?"

"Yes."

Taking his huge erect penis from his boxer shorts he slowly inserts it inside her wet vagina. They both moan out loud at the same time.

"Oh my God, your pussy is so tight."

"Yeah, well it's all yours. Now fuck me like it's the last time you're ever going to have the privilege."

Instantly he begins banging harder and harder. The euphoria surging around his body is intense. He fucks her aggressively, releasing all his pent-up frustration by banging her hard against the desk. The items surrounding Angela begin falling to the floor. Not caring, Lamont is loving the thrill. Lamont then grabs her by the shoulders, fucking her deep. Angela moans, "I'm going to come. I want you to come inside me, baby."

"Okay, baby, I'm going to come right inside that pussy." Banging against her harder and harder he shouts, "I'm coming. Oh my God, I'm coming."

The pair climax together. Lamont feels the surge of semen charge into her, and Angela's body begins to pulsate on his penis. Lamont collapses on top of her, his heart pounding. The pair say nothing as they try and catch their breath.

Peering up at him, Angela smiles. Smiling back, Lamont locks eyes with her. As she brings her hand to her face. Angela starts to laugh. Looking at her and their current situation, Lamont too begins to laugh.

Shaking her head and buttoning her shirt back up, Angela says, "I best go and sort myself out in the bathroom. I hope no one is outside. Look at me, do I have *I've-just-been-fucked* face and hair?"

Laughing, Lamont replies, "What do you think? You've just been fucked by me, of course you have." Reaching over he brushes a strand of hair off her face. "There you go, that's better."

"I need you to go and see if the coast is clear so I can run to the ladies and clean myself up," she says.

The two get dressed and make themselves look as presentable as they possibly can and head towards the door. Placing his finger to his lips, Lamont mimes, "Sshhh..." as he pulls the handle down.

Opening the door ever so slightly, he peers his head through the gap. Almost immediately he sees Alan standing with his briefcase in one hand and a hot coffee in the other. His eyes are wide, like he has just seen a ghost, and his jaw is practically on the floor. He points his finger and mumbles, "You two..."

"Alan, shh..." Lamont says.

Angela rips the door from out of his hand.. With a stern expression on her face she says, "You heard and saw nothing." She then walks off down the corridor and into the ladies bathroom.

"We have no choice but to dismiss you from the Force with immediate effect."

Lamont puts his head down. He knew this was going to happen but hearing the words doesn't make this any easier. Yeah, he might be a bit bullish within his role, but he's a passionate person. His one and only purpose was to have those truly sick individuals, who decide to take the lives of innocent people, put behind bars for life. He had a burning desire to get justice for the deceased, the victims. The child murderers, the worst animals of all, they truly got his back up. It's unfortunate that this suspected child murderer was in fact innocent. Matthew Honey's unbelievable tale of bumps in the night and evil spiritual entities was in fact the truth. Although during the investigation, no one within the Force actually bought into what Matthew Honey was alleging had happened, and the evidence, at times, seemed to suggest that there was a chance Matthew Honey had something to do with his daughter's disappearance and his wife's tragic death, none of the other members of the Force behaved the way Lamont did – intimidating witnesses and trying to get them to lie in their statements, to make Matthew Honey look guilty, along with stalking Matthew and treating him unfairly. The case was stacked against Lamont. And so, even with the defence being put forward by his lawyer that this was an act of desperation to try to get justice for a missing young girl and her murdered mother, it still wasn't enough to save his career. After his behaviour and his outburst today, his superiors, decided that Lamont's uncontrollable temper and highly unprofessional approach is inexcusable.

Sitting back in his chair, Lamont is bewildered and lost for words. He tries to push down the lump in his throat. He then stands and makes his way towards the door to leave the room. Angela and Alan both excuse themselves and follow him.

Walking with his head low and his hand to his face, Lamont is desperately trying to hold back the tears. He doesn't want anyone to know he's weak. He's still fighting the lump at the back of his throat, which is growing bigger by the second. His eyes also well up and his lip quivers slightly. He can't believe he's just lost everything. Just like that, his life has changed dramatically. Five people have determined his fate. He's no longer a member of the Force. He can no longer seek justice for others. He's no longer able to assist with making the world a safer place.

Catching him up, Angela grabs his shoulder and holds him. Squeezing him tightly, she whispers in his ear, "It's okay."

Pulling back, Lamont says nothing and makes his way down the corridor. As he reaches the lifts, he presses the button. The huge metal doors open and he steps inside, wiping his eyes so that the cameras don't catch his tears falling. Just as the doors are about to shut, Angela forces her way through. Standing next to him she says, "I'm not leaving you on your own right now."

"I'm a big boy, Angela, I'll be fine."

"Yes, that might be so, but I just want to stay with you for a moment."

The journey down to the ground floor is a silent one. With a jolt and a *ding* the doors open. Lamont looks up and sees red!

Standing in the reception, acting like he's some sort of hero, is Matthew Honey. Directly at the side of him with his hand on Matthew's shoulder is DCS Terry. Angela says, "Leave it alone. Please don't do anything stupid."

But her words land on deaf ears. Lamont storms out of the lift. Marching after him, Angela grabs his arm and tries to pull him back. Unsuccessful, she says, "Please, just think about this for a second."

"No!" he barks back at her.

Matthew and DCS Terry have their backs to him. They can't see him coming. Furious, he shouts, "Oi... traitor."

DCS Terry drops his arm from Matthew's shoulder and turns around. Seeing Lamont fast approaching, Matthew smirks.

DCS Terry replies, "Come on, pal, let's not fall out."

"Oh, I think we're way beyond falling out. Where the fuck 'ave you been?"

"What you on about?"

"You know exactly what I'm on about. I've been asking for you to back me up for months. Practically begging you to tell the board that I am not what others say I am. I am not a bully."

"Pal, they told me I couldn't come anywhere near or I'd be placed under investigation too. They tied my hands. I wanted to help you, I really did."

Looking to Matthew and seeing a huge smirk upon his face, Lamont can't bite his tongue anymore, "So, you happy now?"

With his face still lighting up Matthew calmly replies, "Ecstatic."

"I should smack that smug look off your face."

"Try me!"

With his smirk growing, Matthew stays calm and continues, "Remember that day I came to the station to adhere to my bail and I said to you that I was going to prove my innocence and have you stripped of your job and ensure that you lose all your power, and you never for a second believed me and told me to watch my back as you laughed? Remember, Monty?"

"Fuck you!"

"Yeah, I thought as much. I'm a man of my word, as you can tell." Walking towards Lamont, Matthew leans to his ear and continues, "Enjoy your sad life. It was a pleasure doing business with you."

Lamont gets hold of Matthew by the scruff of his neck. Angela and DCS Terry grab the pair and split them up. Dragging Matthew towards the lifts, DCS Terry says, "Are you okay?"

"Yeah I've never felt better," Matthew replies as he straightens out his collar.

"I'm going to ruin you, Matthew. You hear me? This isn't the last you've seen of me!" Lamont screams at the top of his lungs.

"Really? You're going to start threatening him in the headquarters? Get a fucking grip," Angela tells Lamont.

Angela drags Lamont out of the building, the security assisting her. Looking back, Lamont sees Matthew in the lift. Just as the doors are about the close, he sees Matthew's face through the gap. Showcasing a huge smirk, Matthew gives him a cheeky wave. No sooner had he seen this the lift doors close shut.

At the top of his lungs Lamont screams, "You scummy bastard!"

CHAPTER 6

I'm Ready!

Phil Parkinson is perched up at the bar in a drunken state. He's looking at his reflection in the mirror behind the bar, engaged in a staring competition with himself.

"Who do you think you're looking at?" he shouts.

He sways on the bar stool and the flimsy seat slides from underneath him and he falls onto his back.

The other customers look at him nervously then begin quietly sniggering under their breath. Looking to her friend, one girl whispers, "That's karma for ya."

Struggling to get himself up off the ground, Phil begins laughing hysterically. He falls back once more, banging his head slightly. Giving up, he shouts to the nearest group, "Oi, can someone do us a favour and pass me down me drink?"

Not a single person looks his way. Phil rolls around laughing. Sitting at the other end of the bar is a young woman dressed head to toe in black. With her long, perfectly straight, dark brown hair, dark brown eyes, plump glossy lips and tanned complexion, this young woman is stunning. She's been watching Phil with an amused expression on her face. Throwing the remainder of her drink to the back of her throat, she slams the glass down on the bar, wipes her mouth on her sleeve and makes her way across to Phil. She bends down and lifts him up.

"Why thank you, kind sir," Phil says. Then, looking to his rescuer he says, "Oh – I – mean – miss." He once again starts laughing to himself.

The woman pulls a face at Phil's second-hand whiskey breath. She wraps one of his arms over her shoulder and drags him to the nearest empty booth. Lying him down she says, "Wait there, I'm going to get you a drink."

"Nice one, I'll have whisky or vodka," Phil slurs.

"You'll have water."

"Oi, don't be a party pooper."

Ignoring his insults, she walks to the bar and gets a glass of water. When she returns, Phil is still in the same position in which she left him. Banging the glass on the table she shouts, "Oi!", but he doesn't move. She puts her fingers in the glass and flicks the cold water onto Phil's face and again shouts, "Oi!"

This time Phil gasps as he shoots up. Wiping his face, he says, "What?"

"You need to drink this water."

"No, I don't, I need a proper drink."

"You won't get one in here, I've already told Davey not to serve you another drink."

"Well, I'll have to go find somewhere that will," Phil replies, attempting to lift himself out of the booth. He fails instantly and his head begins to spin.

"Honestly, drink this water. I promise, you'll start feeling better in around half an hour or so."

Wanting nothing more than for his head to stop spinning, Phil gives in. His hands shaking, he picks up the glass and gulps the water back. Phil immediately regrets this as it comes straight back up as he vomits on the floor. Red with embarrassment, Phil keeps his head under the table, hoping the young woman will disappear. But he sees that her feet aren't about to move anytime soon. Blood has rushed to his head and his temples are now pulsating, creating a surging pain in his eyes. Eventually giving in, Phil lifts his head.

The woman sits with her arms crossed on the table, staring in Phil's direction with a stern look upon her face. She whistles to get the barman's attention and shouts, "Yo, Davey, we need a clean-up over here."

Rolling his eyes, Davey turns to the lad who is collecting glasses from tables and says, "Robbie, go clean that up for us, good lad."

Swaying in his seat and dying of embarrassment, Phil has developed a brain thumping headache.

The woman takes in his expression and laughs. "Hurts like a bitch doesn't it?" she says under her breath.

"Yes," Phil replies, holding his head in his hands. Looking across to her through the gaps in his fingers, he says, "What's your name?"

"Selena," she says, holding out her hand.

Shaking her hand Phil replies, "Phil. Nice to meet you, Selena, and thank you."

"Not a problem, Phil." Smiling she continues, "So, come on, what's a guy like you doing in a bar like this on a Saturday lunchtime?"

"Selena, you really don't want to know."

"That bad huh?"

"Yep."

"You wanna talk about it? Might help to get it off your chest."

"Why are you helping me?" Phil says abruptly.

Laughing slightly, she replies, "Well, I've not seen you about before so you're not a regular and now that I've spoken to you, your accent seems to suggest that you're from up north. Then the way you were knocking them drinks back, you're one hundred percent not a regular day drinker. And then, I saw the wedding band on your hand and thought ah ha, his wife is giving him a hard time. Then I thought if he goes home in this state she's going to give him an even harder time, so why not do my good deed for the day and help you out."

"Huh, your good deed isn't needed here."

"Oh shit, sorry, has your wife already left you?"

"No, Selena, she's dead."

Selena's jaw drops. "Fuck, erm, I wasn't, erm, shit, I'm sorry, man."

"What you sorry for? You didn't put the rope around her neck, I practically did."

With tears forming in his eyes, Phil crumbles.

Selena looks around awkwardly. Her eyes fall to Robbie, who is cleaning the vomit, "Help," she mimes.

Robbie shakes his head and disappears.

Eventually, Phil pulls himself back together. Wiping his swollen red eyes, he says, "I'm sorry, it just gets me every time."

"No, I'm sorry, man, it's my fault, thinking I know everything as per usual. I don't know when to shut my mouth sometimes."

"It's okay you weren't…" Phil trails off as he sees his phone flashing. It's a call from Matthew. He answers it immediately, "Matthew."

"Phil, guess what?"

"What, mate?"

"Monty just got the boot."

"That's great news mate."

"Where are ya? Me and Terry are waiting for you to start the meeting."

"Look I'm gonna 'ave to go. I'll be over there soon."

"Phil, are you in the pub again?" Matthew asks.

"What?"

"You heard me."

"Yeah. Mate, I can't cope. I'm struggling, man."

"Phil, come on, we got this. I know you don't want to hear this, Phil, but she's gone, just like my Lauren. She isn't coming back. The relapse isn't worth it. Drinking will not help you, it will only slow you down."

Phil sniffles.

"We've got to get our kids back," Matthew says in a gentler tone. "Come on, you said you'd die trying with me and that you wanted to get sober. You've been sober a full forty hours clearly you've got it in you to stay sober."

"Yeah, that's before—"

"Phil, get a fucking grip," Matthew interrupts. "This bitch is evil and preys on the weak. You need to get fucking strong and fast. I can't save them all on my own. I need you."

Wiping his face once more, Phil breathes deeply and says, "You're right, mate. I'm ready!"

"That's the spirit. Where are ya?"

"Erm, Selena, what's this pub called?"

"The Scunny."

"Wait, who's Selena?"

"She's a girl that's been looking after me. Got meself in a state again, didn't I."

"Right, get a taxi to Scotland Yard, I know where you are, you're not too far away. We'll start the meeting now and update you when you get here. Be quick, Phil, and try to sober up a little before you get here. Oh, and when you arrive, just sign in and tell that receptionist that you're joining DCS Terry. We've already told her you'll be arriving soon. Once you've signed in, take the lift to the tenth floor. We're in the first big meeting room on your right as you leave the lift."

"Okay. I will do, mate."

"See you soon."

Phil puts the phone down on the side and stands, "Best go and clean up," he says.

"Wait, what was that about?" Selena asks.

"Nothing."

Saying no more, Phil puts his phone back inside his trouser pocket and heads towards the toilets to sort himself out. He walks into the nearest cubicle and begins emptying his bladder. Mid flow, he suddenly hears a familiar nursery rhyme tune. No sooner has this sound circulated around his eardrums than he hears a voice whisper, "Phil."

The voice, the sweet female voice sounds familiar. Confused, Phil shouts, "Hello?" But he gets no reply.

He starts to sway. Assuming he's suffering side effects from the amount of alcohol he's consumed, Phil tries to place his focus back on the task in hand. Once he has finished and flushed the chain, he again hears the nursey rhyme tune and the same female voice whisper, "Phil."

He racks his brain. It almost sounds like... no... it couldn't possibly be. Scratching his head, he opens the cubicle door. Straight ahead of him is the sink area. Above the sinks are multiple grubby mirrors. Seeing his reflection and the state he's in, Phil gets teary eyed. He heads to the sink and splashes freezing cold water in his face. With his head low, he once again hears, "Phil."

He looks up. His jaw drops. It can't be. There's no possible way it can be her. In shock Phil whispers, "How?"

Phil sees his beautiful wife in the mirror. Her face is the same way as it was when he last saw her before he disappeared: stunning, radiant and with a smile from ear to ear. It almost appears as if there's a glow, an angelic gentle glow surrounding her. Phil doesn't freak out. Instead, he slowly leans forward. Crying, he reaches out his arms and says, "My queen. I'm so sorry."

"Don't be sorry. Join me," Alice responds.

"Join you where?"

"Join me in the afterlife, my king."

"But the…"

"Sshh… no buts."

Phil is both relieved and confused. Seeing his wife as she once was, her natural smile and her radiant beauty, is enticing him closer. He touches the glass in an attempt to stroke his wife's face. But no sooner have his fingertips grazed the mirror than she suddenly disappears.

"No, Alice, wait, don't go," he shouts. "Alice, no, no, no, no, no, come back. Please, I can't lose you again. I'll join y—"

Phil falls silent as the lights abruptly switch off. Standing in complete darkness, Phil feels as though he's no longer alone. Fear takes over his body. He's frozen. His heart's beating at a rapid rate. Hearing a click come from the direction of the doorway, Phil whispers, "Hello…?"

There is no response. He puts his hand in his pocket and pulls out his mobile phone. Phil has never felt so scared in all his life. Turning on the torch, he reluctantly glances back at the mirror. He breathes a sigh of relief when he sees it's empty. But then he senses a huge presence looming over his shoulder, and it's not of the welcoming kind. He turns slowly… and sees that there's no one there. Suddenly a dark shadow glides past him. Now desperate to get out of the toilets, he attempts to step forward. But he's shocked to discover that he can't move his legs.

"Help!" he screams.

No one appears to rescue him and now he starts to really panic. He begins to hear a familiar tune circulating and gets an urge to look back at the mirror. Turning, he sees Alice is once again standing there. He's desperate to break free and save her, but he still can't move. Feeling helpless and frustrated, he begins crying and calling out, "Alice, please, just wait for me, I'm coming to save you. Please, don't go anywhere. Just wait for me."

He struggles to lift his legs, to no avail. Frustration takes over and tears fall from his face. Liquid gushes from his nose. He wants nothing more than to get to his queen right now. Alice begins to sing, "Ring a' Ring o' Roses – their souls are mine. Ring a' Ring o' Roses – they belong to the dark side."

As the final word is sung, a black substance begins gushing from Alice's mouth and trickles from the surroundings of her eye sockets. She laughs hysterically. Covering his ears, to protect himself, Phil screams out in pain. Suddenly, the insane laughter stops. Slowly removing his hands, Phil looks back to the mirror. Alice is still there, except she's slowly looking less like Alice with every second that passes. With a painful expression upon her face, Alice reaches out her arms and pleads, "Phil – please – don't let her take me again. Please, Phil, save my soul."

Now the evil entity reveals herself in the mirror. Alice is no longer Alice. Peering at Phil through the gap in her hair is Jezebel!

"Ring a' Ring o' Roses – their souls are mine. Ring a' Ring o' Roses – stay away from the dark side." Jezebel throws herself out of the mirror and screams, *"Essere avvertito!"*

Screaming out with fear, Phil drops his phone on the floor. Suddenly the lights come on. Standing in the doorway is a slightly confused drunken male. He stares at Phil.

"You alright, man?" he says.

Opening his eyes, Phil sees that the demonic figure has gone. He looks at the mirror. There's nothing but a reflection of himself. Pale, delirious and with his hands shaking, Phil says, "Yeah, erm, too much to drink mate." He's relieved to find he can once more move his legs and turns to leave.

As he reaches the door he feels a tap on his shoulder. Phil whirls around and pushes the man to the ground.

"Oi, what the fuck are you doing? I was just giving you your phone back. Knobhead."

"Shit, sorry," says Phil. "I'm so sorry. Thank you."

Grabbing his phone, Phil puts his head down and rushes out of the pub.

"Phil!" shouts Selena.

Without stopping he shouts, "What?"

"Just stop a minute, man, I just want to see if you're alright," she replies breathlessly.

"I'm fine. Go away!"

"What's your problem, man?"

"I don't have a problem when people leave me the fuck alone."

"Fine, have it your way. I don't give a shit anyway. Who the fuck even are you?"

Feeling bad, Phil stops. As he turns, he sees Selena walking back to the pub. She's shaking her head.

"Selena, I'm sorry. I'm just a mess at the minute. I'm seeing things and I can't get my head straight."

Selena stops and turns around, "I'm just trying to help, that's all."

"I know, I'm grateful, really I am."

Selena walks back to Phil, grabs his phone and puts her number in it, "Just in case you wanna chat, I'm here." Selena then walks back into the pub.

CHAPTER 7

The Surprise Call

Sitting in the oversized airy meeting room on the tenth floor in Scotland Yard, Matthew and DCS Terry are deep in discussion. On high alert, sat with his back up straight, Matthew is engrossed in what DCS Terry is saying. With a notepad in front of him and a pen firmly grasped in his hand, Matthew's arrived prepared and has been taking notes vigorously. Desperate to get help, he's over the moon with DCS Terry's offer.

"Okay, so I know we've covered a lot of the stuff that I have access to on the system here, which you must promise to keep to yourself," DCS Terry says.

Matthew nods.

"And we've also covered how you believe this entity, Jezebel, is doing what it's doing and why it's doing it. So, what I think we need to work out now, is how are we going to defeat it when we do locate it, right?"

"Yeah," Matthew replies.

"Do you have any inclination or possible suggestion on how we might be able to complete this successfully?"

Breathing deeply, Matthew doesn't answer the question. He begins twiddling the pen he holds as he stares at the floor in a daze. Unsure if he should tell DCS Terry what Reverend Andrew Read told him a while ago or keep it to himself, Matthew's feeling apprehensive about this officer of the law's possible reaction.

Don't tell him, the incessant voice inside his head whispers.

He's an officer of the law. You're basically telling him you'll be committing murder. Really, do you want to admit that you're premeditating murder to a Detective? That isn't a smart move, Matthew. You just keep your mouth shut. Remember, you can't trust him, he's just like the other copper, Monty. And, who's to say this copper ain't in on it with Monty and that they're now both trying to set you up? This could be his revenge. Do not open your mouth, it's safer that way. Listen to me, stay quiet.

Waving his hand, DCS Terry says, "Erm, hello. Matthew, you okay?"

Snapping out of his trance Matthew says, "Yeah – sorry. Yeah, I'm fine."

"Huh, thought we'd lost you for a second then."

"Yeah, sorry. No, I'm alright."

"So...?"

"So what?" Matthew responds.

"Do you have any idea how we might be able to defeat this entity?"

"Terry, I think I do, but I can't tell you."

"Why not?"

"I just can't."

"Matthew, whatever is said in this room is kept between us. You're not even supposed to be here. Honestly, it will go no further."

"Let me ask you this, then: why are you helping me?"

"I told you, that sick bitch has cost me a lot in my life. I almost lost my job and I've lost a lot of great colleagues. I've seen good, hardworking people lose everything. It's the least I can do for them."

"So you're not trying to frame me like Monty?"

"No – not at all," DCS Terry says with genuine look of shock plastered across his face.

Don't do it, the voice again whispers.

Shaking his head, Matthew overcomes his nerves and decides he's going to take the risk and be honest. After all, no crime has been committed by just telling him what he knows, "There is one thing," Matthew says as he gets up from his seat. He then puts his hand in his trouser pocket. Retrieving the silver cross that Reverend Andrew Read gave him, he puts it on the table and seats himself.

"What's that?" DCS Terry says, picking the item up.

"I'm not quite sure, if I'm honest," Matthew replies. "I was given this months ago by a Reverend I know. He said that I would…" Pausing, Matthew takes a deep breath, "…need to stab their hearts with this."

"What? Whose hearts?"

"He didn't say, but if I had to guess, I'd think he meant Jezebel's, Eve's, and anyone else's that she has tainted using her evil."

"Wow, that's deep. Like murder?" DCS Terry says immediately.

See, I told you, the voice says.

"Honestly, I don't know, Terry. I'm hoping it will somehow break, like, the curse or something, but I really don't know. I've been carrying it round in my pocket since he gave it to me just in case I might catch up with them one day. But then the reality hits and I begin questioning myself. Like, can I really do this? Can I really stab my daughter's heart? Well, anyone's heart? Jezebel's, for sure! I'd kill that bitch in a millisecond, and I don't care that I'm saying that to you, even with your position; plus, I'm certain her heart is black anyway. But, my daughter? Phil's children? And anyone else she's tainted? Really, stab their hearts? When I think about it, I just don't know if I can do that." Getting frustrated, Matthew continues, "I just keep mulling it over in my head and I know I…" Before Matthew can finish what he is saying there's a knock at the door.

"Come in!" DCS Terry shouts.

Seeing Phil peer his head through the gap in the door, Matthew releases a heavy sigh. Part of this is relief to know that his friend is okay, and part is that he's relieved to get off topic of potentially having to commit murder. Matthew smiles, "Phil, you made it."

Making his way into the room, Phil hangs his head.

"Here, sit next to me," Matthew says as he pulls out the chair to his right.

"Hi. Phil, nice to see you again," DCS Terry says, putting out his hand.

"Hi," Phil says shyly, returning the handshake before he sits.

"I think the last time we saw each other was a week or so after the unfortunate events took place with your wife and children."

"Yeah, I think it was," Phil says with an expression of sadness, his voice low.

Wanting to update Phil, Matthew says, "You haven't missed much, we have been discussing…" But again, Matthew is interrupted as his phone begins ringing. He doesn't recognise the number. With the phone still ringing he asks, "Where's zero, one, three, zero, three?"

"No idea," Phil responds.

"It's okay. Just excuse me for a second." Getting up from his seat, Matthew makes his way to the other side of the meeting room, "Hello, Matthew Honey speaking." There's silence at the other end. "Erm, hello, is anybody there?"

A gentle female voice is then heard, "Matthew?"

"Yes, this is Matthew. Who's calling, please?"

"You don't know me, but I've been following your journey for some time now."

"Who is this?" Matthew questions.

"My name is Sandra."

"Okay – what is it I can help you with, Sandra?"

"It is I who can help you, Matthew."

"What are you trying to imply, Sandra? Is this another joke call? I thought I'd gotten past this."

"No, it's not. Look, I can't talk over the phone – she hears me in my thoughts."

"Who hears your thoughts?"

"I cannot say her name. Please, I need you to come and visit me at my store. Will you please visit me? I have information that is vital for you. I can help you get her back," she says quietly.

Ready to take all the help he can, Matthew dashes back across the room and grabs his notepad and pen, "Yeah, sure, I will come visit you. What's your address?"

"I'm on High Street, Lyminge, in Folkstone. The shop has a sign above it that says, 'Magic is Within'."

Looking to his watch, Matthew replies, "Okay, so it's two thirty now, I think I can get there in the next two hours, is that okay?"

"No, you mustn't come now, it's daytime! She might know that I've spoken to you. Come in the early hours of the morning, around three a.m. She is always busy with the children around that time."

"Who might know that you've spoken to me?"

The phone goes silent. Matthew doesn't want to say the name of the entity he believes Sandra is talking about in case it freaks her out and he loses the only potential lead he might have. Desperate to get her to talk, he pleads one final time, "Sandra, please, you have to tell me what you are talking about?"

"Just promise me you will be here at three a.m.?" Sandra says urgently.

"I promise."

As soon as Matthew says the words, the call is ended. Looking to his phone and scratching his head, Matthew has no clue what has just happened or why, but he's certain it could be important.

"Who was it?" DCS Terry asks.

"Some lady called Sandra."

"What did she want?"

"I don't know, but I think she might know where they are."

Phil jumps from his seat, "The kids?"

"I don't know, to be honest, Phil, but I think so."

"What are we waiting for, then?" Phil barks.

"We can't go now, she said something about going at three a.m. because she's always busy with the children then."

"Busy with the children? Well, will we not wake them up if we're banging at the door at three a.m?"

"I don't know. I'm just as confused as you are and I was the one on the call."

"Erm, okay, so I guess we're going at three a.m., then?" Phil says, appearing eager.

Looking to DCS Terry, Matthew says, "Fancy coming with and giving us a lift?"

"Yeah, I could check it out with ya. Where is it?"

Looking at his notepad, Matthew recites what he has written down, "Some shop on the High Street in Lyminge called 'Magic is Within'."

"Okay," DCS Terry replies, "I'm in."

Smiling, Matthew's confident. This might be the lead they need to get his daughter back. With a deep breath, he whispers, "Eve, I'm coming for you, darling."

CHAPTER 8

The Whisper

The Moycullen Nunnery is barely visible under the cover of the night. A thick grey mist has developed and is taking over the grounds. Not a sound can be heard. The silence is deadly. An unnerving, oppressive energy reigns supreme. The nocturnal animals that prowl the forest are too intimidated to approach the nunnery. Something evil is lurking and they can sense it.

Inside the nunnery, the sisters are all sleeping. Well, all, that is, except one. Mother Superior Sister Kathryn is praying inside the candlelit chapel alone. She's on her knees with her head low and her hands grasped tightly together, resting against her head. She squeezes her rosary beads as she prays to the Lord for answers and protection. Believing she has a strong relationship with God, Sister Kathryn is requesting that her residents and sisters are shielded from evil.

Trusting in the mercy of the Lord, Sister Kathryn prays out loud, "Father, I thank you for the closeness of our relationship throughout the years. Father, first of all, I wish to pray for those who are sick, suffering and are in need of help. Father, I wish to pray for my sisterhood and the children. Father, I now pray for myself. Father, please help, I fear something unholy has entered these walls. Father, if we are bound by evil, I pray for protection of our young. I pray for protection of my sisters. I pray for them to be blinded and not see the evil that can lie within. I pray not for protection of myself but of them first. Father, I trust in you. Father, I selflessly sacrifice myself for my sisters and our children. If you will allow me to see the evil, if you allow me, Father, I will do all that I can within my power to save us from evil. I ask for nothing in return but for you to stand by my side. Father, I am your child. Guide me so I can save the lives of many, even if this means I am to be the sacrifice."

Sister Kathryn jumps at a loud sound coming from the confession booth. A horrific, spine-trembling sound, like nails on a chalk board. Her heart is racing and she can't finish her prayer. Standing up and breathing deeply, she bravely makes her way across to the confession booth. As she gets closer, taking one tiny step at a time, Sister Kathryn hears a whisper. A breeze gently brushes her face, the freezing temperature making the tiny hairs on her skin stand to attention. Sister Kathryn doesn't let this deter her. She wants to find out who or what is in the confession booth. She comes to a stop a few feet away. Her heart is beating fiercely against her chest and the horrific scratching is getting fiercer. Kissing her beads and placing her hand to her head, lower chest and on each shoulder, she whispers, "Father, please protect me."

She reaches out to the handle, but as she does the scratching stops! She hears, "Kathryn…" and she jumps, almost tripping over her own feet.

"Who's there?" she shouts.

There is no response. The only sound she can hear is the echoing of her own voice. The scratching sound returns with a vengeance. Tears of fear fall from Sister Kathryn's eyes. Holding out the cross on her rosary beads she bravely shouts, "Show yourself, coward!"

No sooner has she shouted these words than the door to the confession booth bursts open and a huge gust of wind knocks her to the ground. She bangs her head as she lands. Sister Kathryn begins drifting in and out of consciousness. As she closes her eyes she hears a voice in her mind. A voice she's never heard before but that she instantly fears, "They will all die if you fight. Your sisters' blood will be on your hands. Be warned – I now own every soul within these walls."

Fifty children of all different ages are tucked up tightly inside their beds asleep. In the middle of the room, one of the youngsters becomes restless in her sleep. She struggles with her bedsheets, then shouts at the top of her voice, "No, come back!" She sobs, then says, "Mummy, no! Don't go into the forest. Come back! Mummy, no, no, no don't leave me here, I'm scared."

The dorm room door creaks open and a flicker of candlelight comes from the hallway. Sister Jennifer peers around the door. She locates the source of the cries and rushes to the little girl's bedside. She releases her from the bedsheets and cradles her, "Sshhh, Rita, it was just a bad dream. You're going to be okay," Sister Jennifer whispers, planting a kiss on her head.

Rita sobs herself back to sleep. Tucking her in tightly, Sister Jennifer once again kisses her on the head and makes her way towards the door. Glancing back into the room, she sees all is as it should be. Before leaving the room, Sister Jennifer whispers, "Goodnight children." Then she gently closes the door behind her.

But all is not as it should be in the dorm room. A sudden vibration shakes the bedframes. Tendrils of grey mist seep through the gaps around the door and the window frames, coating the room. This can only mean one thing: evil has arrived!

The mist intertwines with the furniture and surrounds the children, forcefully restraining them. Content, the mist calls for its owner. No sooner has the command been made, a dreary humming initiates and a dulcet voice sings, "Ring a' Ring o' Roses – your soul is mine. Ring a' Ring o' Roses – you've been chosen for the dark side."

When the final word has been sung, dark figures appear in each corner of the room. In their true demonic form are Jezebel, Eve, Lewis, Freddie, Terence and Rupert. Their appearance is horrific. They drag their feet as they make their way towards the children's beds, smearing a black substance that drips from their cracked grey skin across the floor. As they each take a position beside a bed, they begin to implement their midnight possession. In unison they sing: "Ring a' Ring o' Roses – your soul is mine…"

Suddenly the children sit up in bed. Their identity has been tainted and they're each a mirror reflection of the evil that lies within.

Standing in the doorway, her head held low, Jezebel peers through the gap in her hair. She stares as her evil spreads around the room, welcoming new members to her demonic empire. Licking her lips, she shouts, *"Salire!"*

She raises her arms and, one by one, the children begin to rise from their beds.

Jezebel's time is coming!

CHAPTER 9

The Invitation

It's almost three a.m. and the rain is falling fiercely from the sky, collecting in huge puddles on the uneven ground. The odd passing vehicle is creating waves of water.

"How do you want to do this?" DCS Terry asks.

"I think you should wait here and me and Phil should go in. I don't want to startle her with too many people, she might not speak." Trying to explain the logic behind his thought process, Matthew continues, "The likely chances are, if she knows about me, she will know about Phil."

"What, you want me to go in with you?" Phil says nervously.

Fed up with Phil's wimpy ways, Matthew rolls his eyes and says, "Phil, sort it out. Of course I want you to come in with me. Your kids are missing, too. I need another pair of eyes on the place in case I miss something."

Taking a deep breath in, Phil says, "Okay. I'll come in with you."

"Terry, you just stay in the car and keep the engine running. Judging from the outside of this place, I'm guessing we're not going to be hanging around here too long."

"You sure you don't want me to come in and leave Phil here? He seems like he's going to be too nervous to help." Turning he says, "I mean, look at him. Really, what's he gonna do?"

Smiling at DCS Terry's minor insult about Phil's cowardly ways, Matthew replies, "I know what you're saying, but honestly, I think it's best you just stay here. Phil's gonna have to get a grip, aren't you lad?" Matthew says as he peers at the back of the car where Phil sits.

"Look, I'm not being funny, yeah, but this is nerve wracking for me. Take the piss all you want, but you know I'm trying to conquer my drinking at the moment so I'm on edge about everything."

"I know, I'm sorry, I shouldn't make fun of you." Realising he has been too harsh, Matthew tries a gentle approach. "Look, mate, come on, this is just the first challenge. It's just a friendly lady who wants to help us. What's so scary about that?"

"Nothing," Phil whispers with his head low.

Matthew continues, "See. So, I'm gonna run over and I'll signal you when I get to the doorway – okay?"

"Okay."

Matthew opens the car door. His face is instantly blasted by the fast blowing wind. The temperature is freezing cold and the rain turns into solid rocks of hail, creating unbearable momentary pain on Matthew's skin. He desperately attempts to shield himself with his coat as he leaves the comfort of DCS Terry's car. Matthew moans in agony as he is pelted at full force in the face. Soaking wet, he sees the empty doorway of the shop and the sign that reads 'Magic is Within' positioned above it and runs there to take shelter. He wipes his red raw face as he looks around and signals for Phil to join him. Seeing him appear from the shadows of the bus shelter where DCS Terry has parked, Matthew waves his arms, "Hurry, Phil!" he shouts.

Phil runs over and hops inside the doorway. "Fuck's sake, man, where did that come from?"

"I don't know but that hurt."

Matthew leans against the door and is caught off guard when it creaks open, causing him to stumble backwards. Puzzled, Matthew and Phil step back onto the pavement, shielding themselves with their coats once more, they watch as the solid dark oak wooden door slowly opens.

"Did you open that?" Matthew asks.

"No," Phil says.

Nervous and unsure of what to do next, Matthew reaches over and places his hand on the ivory doorknob. He peers his head through the slight gap and says, "Hello?"

He gets no reply.

When the door unexpectedly flings itself open, Matthew appears to be dragged inside the building. The door then slams shut, leaving Phil unaided on the other side. Inside in the darkness, Matthew hears Phil kick the door and scream at the top of his voice, "Matthew! Can you hear me? Matthew, I'm coming, mate."

Deciding to put him out of his misery, Matthew turns the knob and eases the door open.

"Fucking hell, mate, you had me worried then," Phil says.

"You shit yourself then," Matthew replies, laughing.

"Ah, don't take the piss. I thought you were gone, mate."

"What, me? You think they're gonna take me that easy? Not a chance." Opening the door wide, Matthew says, "Come on, then, let's see what this is about."

He turns and makes his way down the dark hallway. Phil follows. No sooner have they taken four steps inside the haunted-looking building than the door bangs shut behind them. They're surrounded by darkness.

"Sandra, are you there?" Matthew says.

There's no reply.

"Sandra, it's me, Matthew Honey. Can you hear me?"

Again, nothing but silence.

"I think we should go look for her."

Phil's breathing suddenly becomes heavy, "I'm about to have a panic attack. I think we should leave."

"Just breathe deeply. Come on, follow me."

Matthew and Phil begin reaching out in front of them, feeling their way around. Matthew touches one of the walls and follows its trail, arriving at what he believes is another door. But with no light it's almost impossible for him to gauge his surroundings. Feeling for a doorknob, Matthew whispers, "Aye, Phil, where are ya?"

"Over here, mate."

"I think I've found another door."

"Okay, I'm coming now."

Matthew feels Phil's hand on his shoulder as he turns the doorknob. The door creaks open. He puts his head through the gap and shuffles one step forward.

"Hello," he says quietly.

No response.

"Is anybody in here?" he asks.

Still nothing.

Matthew shuffles back into the hallway and reaches out his hands, "Phil?"

"Yeah, mate."

"I can't see a fucking thing – but I think we should go inside this room."

"What? Are you mad? Not a chance. We're already technically trespassing as she didn't even let us in – we've just walked in."

"No, we're not. One, we've got a copper outside to back us up. Two, we got a call asking us to come here. And three, the door opened by itself – that's practically an invitation."

"After all the freaky goings-on, if you think I'm stepping even one toe inside that creepy ass room, you've got another thing coming."

"Ha, you pussy. Well, I'm going in."

"Yep, you do that. I'll see you on the other side when I'm dead too, mate."

"Oh, shut it, you wimp."

Matthew pushes the door open fully and a huge creak echoes throughout the space. Much like the entrance to the building, the room is also pitch-black inside. And there is an unbearable strong stench of mould. Putting his sleeve over his nose, Matthew desperately tries not to throw up as the horrific odour makes its way up his nostrils. Unable to see what's in front of him, he puts one foot in front of the other, getting further into the dark space. Matthew's nerves are getting the better of him. All his senses are heightened. Feeling a tickle on his neck, Matthew jumps and screams out.

"Mate, you alright?" Phil shouts.

"Yeah, I'm fine. It's just a bit… dark. It's messing with my head. You know how it is."

"Mate, I've got an idea! You got your phone?" Phil asks.

"Yeah, why?"

"Use the torch on it."

Feeling somewhat stupid as he didn't think of this, Matthew takes his phone out of his pocket and puts on the torch. As it lights up the room, Matthew is shocked by what he sees. The walls are black, the floor is black and there isn't a window in sight. He's standing in the centre of a very dark room. It almost looks like a bottomless pit. Directly in front of him are three closed doors. The only difference on each of these is the doorknobs. One is red, one is gold and the other is black. Amazed, confused and unsure of what to do next, Matthew says, "Phil, you gotta come see this."

"No thanks, I'm good here," Phil says from outside the room.

"Phil, stop being a dick and come here."

Phil says nothing. Then Matthew hears him muttering under his breath, "You don't need to go in this scary ass room to prove anything to anyone. You're okay out here. Just don't listen to him. It's okay to be afraid. It's oka—"

"Oi, dickhead, do it for your kids," Matthew bellows, interrupting his mini pep-talk. "Stop being stupid and get your arse in here."

Phil steps hesitantly into the room. As soon as he's inside, the door slams shut and locks. Phil yelps, runs over to Matthew and clings to him.

"What the fuck, man? Get off me," Matthew says, pushing him off.

"Are you taking the piss? Why the fuck did I let you talk me into coming inside this building?" Phil barks.

"Shut up moaning like a little baby and take a look at this." Shinning his torch towards the doors, Matthew continues, "What do you think it means?"

"What?"

"Look at the handles. They're all different."

"Well, I can tell you this: I ain't stepping inside any one of them doorways to find out."

Rolling his eyes, Matthew says, "Phil, will you for one second stop thinking about yourself and remember the fucking reason we are here."

"Mate, are you being serious? I don't recall going into scary mother fucking buildings that have freaky ass opening and closing doors part of any reason why we're doing this."

"That's because you're a dumbass. What do you think a demon's main aim is?"

"Erm, obviously, kill people."

"For fuck's sake! Talk about stating the obvious. Yes, well done, brownie points for you." Rolling his eyes, Matthew continues, "They play games. A demon wants to fuck with your head. They want to tear you up mentally, weaken you, kill you and take over your soul. That way they can then do whatever they please with you. I'm telling you, Phil, this is a sign. This is part of the process. We are meant to be here. Now do us a favour: stop being a pussy and play the fucking game with me?"

But before Phil has time to reply, a female voice says, "I've been expecting you both."

Matthew grins, ecstatic because he has been proven right. He's excited to play the game, and yet at the same time, he's anxious.

"Nar, I don't like this, mate," Phil says, sounding shaken.

"What's it to be?" the voice says. "I have information for you. One door leads to the answers you desire. Another door leads to tainted trails. And the final door leads to your instant death. You must now choose. You have thirty seconds to decide or your fate will be selected for you."

"Matthew, I can't do this, mate," Phil says, climbing all over him.

"Oh my God, Phil – just do me a favour, stand there and shut ya mouth whilst I try and work this out."

"Mate…"

"Honestly, Phil, I said shh!" Trying to work out the riddle, Matthew begins muttering to himself, "So, one will lead to…what was it? That's it – answers. The other leads to games. And the other leads to death." Consumed by his thoughts, Matthew doesn't see the tiny spot of light appear.

Tapping him on the shoulder, Phil says, "Erm, mate, look."

"What, Phil?"

Looking across the way, Matthew sees the light flickering on the red doorknob. His inner voice tells him this is the one. In a trance, Matthew walks towards the door. Without hesitation he twists the doorknob. As the door creaks open, they're met by darkness.

"Mate, can you smell that?"

"Urgh, yeah, it's making me feel sick."

"It smells like animal crap and cats. Seriously, what the fuck is in this room?"

Shielding their noses, Matthew and Phil slowly make their way further into the room. Hearing a loud screech, Matthew jumps. An old lady appears right before his eyes. Her silver hair is hanging heavy on either side of her face. Her features are wrinkled, and her eyes have dark rings around them. She has at least twenty cats circling her around her feet. Looking to Matthew she says, "You chose well. Thank you for your trust."

Unsure of what to say, Matthew simply replies, "Erm, you're welcome."

"Matthew, I'm so glad you could make it. You too, Phil."

Standing directly behind Matthew, Phil peers his head round, "Thank you. I think," he whispers.

Sandra grabs Matthew's arm and says, "You see, it's the voices, they won't rest. They insist that I speak to you. Come, come quickly, we can't be long or she might find out."

Sandra then drags Matthew inside the room. She claps her hands and the lights come on. There are fully grown cats everywhere. The walls are papered with news articles. Most of these have Matthew, Lauren and Evelyn-Jade Honey's faces on them. And there are multiple missing children posters and a great many drawings, doodles and scribblings of the same dark and dangerous-looking entity. Scattered around the room are paintings of children with black eyes who appear to be crying black tears and drawings of nuns galore. Matthew is lost for words as he tries to take in his surroundings.

"Phil, get in here," Sandra shouts. "I said we must be quick!"

Phil cautiously enters the room. Once again, as soon as he steps inside the doorway, the door slams shut behind him. Walking to her desk, she begins faffing around with some papers, quietly muttering to herself.

"Excuse me, Sandra, what information do you have for us?" Matthew says.

Sandra stops what she's doing. Passing a handful of crumpled-up worn-looking papers to Matthew, she puts her finger to her lip.

Confused, Matthew scans through them. They are drawings of woods and lakes.

"Sandra, why are we here? What do you know about our children?"

Getting agitated, Sandra begins tugging at her clothes and smacking herself in the head, "I can't…"

"It's okay, you don't have to tell us. Just give me a clue, maybe," Matthew says.

"You don't understand."

"What don't I understand, Sandra? Talk to me."

"Not you. The voices in my head don't understand, she's always listening. She listens to my thoughts, my words. The only thing she can't get access to are my drawings."

"Who… Je—"

"Don't call her name!" Sandra shouts.

"What exactly do you know?" Matthew questions.

"I know everything. I've been following you for a while, Matthew."

"Me?"

"Yes, you," Sandra replies with a stern voice. "Around nineteen months ago, I had a spiritual awakening. Through my psychic abilities, I removed myself from my physical form and submitted myself to the spiritual universe. Opening the portal, I was welcomed in, as I often am. But on this particular occasion I came across a warning. A missing child, but not just any child: this child had been chosen by an impure entity. Named *the chosen one*, I saw the girl's face and nothing more. That experience sent constant chills down my spine every time I thought about it. This girl will be capable of the most sinister of things."

"What are you trying to say?" Matthew interrupts.

"Nothing, I'm not trying to imply anything, Matthew. It's just, I came across a news article online that was about your missing daughter – Eve. As soon as I saw her face in the picture, I knew that was the girl I'd seen."

"I'm not sure I like where you're going with this, Sandra," Matthew says.

Taking a deep breath in Sandra again speaks, "I cannot say the obvious, but I have been tracking them."

"You do know where they are, don't you?"

Suddenly, looking extremely distressed, Sandra begins throwing more and more drawings at Matthew, "Ireland," she whispers.

"Huh? What did you say? Ireland?"

Sandra screams and grabs her head.

Phil runs straight to the door and starts pulling on the handle. He desperately tries to kick it open but it's not budging an inch. Sandra falls to the ground and curls up into a ball. Rushing to her aid, Matthew attempts to comfort this fragile looking old lady, but as soon as he arrives at her body he's immediately thrown across the room by an invisible energy surrounding her.

"Leave now before you get hurt!" she bellows.

"Sandra…"

As she turns her head, Matthew sees her features are changing. Her face is sinking into the bony structure of her skull. Her jaw swings open and she groans, "I said leave."

As soon as she has spoken the door opens. Grabbing what drawings he can, Matthew rushes out of the room. Phil is already halfway down the hall. They run out of the original door they came through and stand outside in the street, trying to catch their breath. The solid dark oak door slams shut with a bang and locks.

"Phil, what if that evil bitch is in there with our kids?"

"Doubt it, mate."

"No – when I was about to say her name Sandra was afraid. I could see the fear in her eyes. Phil, I know it, she's in there. Quick, we can't waste any time, help me kick this door down. We have to get back inside."

But, just as Matthew and Phil begin kicking at the door, they're both instantly thrown back. Picking themselves up, they see that the door's gone. Standing in its place is a solid brick wall. It's as though the doorway never existed.

CHAPTER 10

You Knew Your Fate

Sandra lies unconscious, curled up on the floor. Suddenly her body is thrown across the room like a rag doll, then dragged and positioned up against the wall. As her head hits the brick, Sandra wakes. She's unable to cry or scream out for help as her face has become even more disfigured. Against her will, her arms are stretched out either side and her legs are shut tight, her body forming a cross. Her head is slumped. Sandra hears the persistent voices circulating inside her mind once more. She's now fully aware of what's to come. Sandra knows her fate. As soon as she has accepted this, Sandra's frail body begins to spin uncontrollably.

A thick, dark grey mist seeps into the room. The arrival of this deceitful element can only mean one thing: Jezebel has arrived. As it takes over the space, the mist begins taunting the cats in the room. Meowing, they cower in the corner together. As Sandra continues to spin rapidly, the mist eventually reaches her body. It caresses her skin and she comes to an abrupt halt upside down. The blood rushes to her head.

She hears, "Ring a' Ring o' Roses…"

She cannot move, call out or even cry. Aware of her imminent death, Sandra is terrified. She begins to choke and her eyes slowly protrude from their sockets. A huge gust of wind blows through the room, ripping all the paintings and articles off the wall. Paper flies everywhere, scattering all over the floor. It's time. The mist calls for its owner. Thick black blood trickles down the walls. It coats Sandra, travelling through her nostrils, mouth and eye sockets. Her features change. Sandra is no longer Sandra. She's now Jezebel. Her eyes shoot open. They are blood red. Jezebel has taken full reign over Sandra's body and soul. Sandra's head twists in a three-hundred-and-sixty-degree turn. She then drops to the floor and begins crawling across the room to the desk. Standing, she stares at the mirror. Remaining in full control of Sandra's body, Jezebel allows Sandra's soul to appear in the reflection.

"You knew I'd find you. Like a moth to a flame, you just couldn't resist. You knew your fate. You knew what would bring you to your death, and yet you couldn't stay quiet, could you? You just couldn't keep those voices down. Aw, what a shame. The powers of a psychic. The worst thing you ever did was tune into my universe. You tuned into my dark side. You signed your own death certificate the minute you became obsessed with the Honeys. Not only did you invade my mind – when you tuned into my universe, you saw my face and you saw her face, my chosen one. Well, I think we both know I saw yours, too. Remember, everything leaves a trail, especially in the spiritual universe. Now, Sandra, there is one way you might get to live. I want the truth. You told them where we are, didn't you?"

In the reflection a single tear slowly travels down Sandra's cheek. She seals her fate and lies, "No."

"Oh, how noble of you, or should I say stupid of you."

Suddenly, Eve appears behind Jezebel in her true demonic form.

Her eyes wide, Sandra shouts, "Eve, I know you can hear me, your da—"

But before she even has time to finish her sentence, Jezebel leaves Sandra's body and Eve slits her throat. Thick blood immediately gushes down Sandra's chest from the gaping wound. Sandra's body slumps to the floor. Her hands go to her throat as she desperately tries to stop the blood from leaving her body. She gasps for air. But there's simply no hope. Blood is spouting everywhere. Leaning over Sandra's face, Eve licks her blood with her black course tongue and then spits it back at Sandra. She then takes the black substance from one of her own wounds and rubs it on Sandra's head in an upside-down cross.

"Hiding behind these walls, thinking I wouldn't find you in the dark. Ha, you mistake me for a fool. I am Jezebel. No one will defeat me. I don't know why you tried. She is mine, she always was mine and she always will be mine. You would have been wise to work that out."

Standing proudly at the side of her owner, Eve laughs as she watches Sandra take her last breath. No longer containing a soul, Sandra's body lies on the ground, covered in blood. Her lifeless eyes remain wide open. Content, both Jezebel and Eve disappear.

CHAPTER 11

One Image Can Change Everything

"I promise to always protect you. Your daddy promises to always protect you. I don't know your fate – but what I do know is that I will never stop loving you. I know that you will always be my priority. You are my best friend and I know I can tell you anything. Honey, my darling Honey, today marks two whole weeks since you entered the world. You are so precious. You are a part of something even bigger than me. I never knew what love was. And then along came you. My beautiful baby girl, my Honey Parkinson. You're so precious. You're so beautiful. Please never fear me. I know you are pure. I feel your purity. You are not tainted and I will make sure you stay this way."

Staring at her daughter with nothing but admiration and love, this young brand-new mummy couldn't have embraced motherhood more if she tried – Eve's a natural. Stroking her baby's face, she continues to whisper to her daughter, "I know I might not get it right all the time. But Honey, my darling, I need to confide in you. I can't tell anyone else." Eve looks around the room to ensure she's alone, then continues, "I think I was another person. I think we have another family. I saw an image and it was someone who I believe might be my dad – your grand-daddy. I saw him, I heard his—"

Hearing a creak coming from the floorboards outside her room, Eve stops speaking. Suddenly the doorknob turns and the door creaks open. Peering into her room is Sister Elisabeth.

"I have come for the baby."

"No, you have not. Your help is not needed here."

"But Sister Jesselle insists."

Making her way across to Eve, Sister Elisabeth reaches out her arms to take baby Honey from her.

"Sister Elisabeth, move away now! Or I will hurt you. Let it be known that no one is taking my baby from me."

Ignoring her, Sister Elisabeth attempts to pull the baby out of Eve's arms. True to her word, Eve puts up one heck of a fight and slaps Sister Elisabeth across the face. Stumbling back, Sister Elisabeth becomes angry. She charges towards Eve and baby Honey.

Engulfed by an almighty rage, Eve transforms into her true demonic form. Sister Elisabeth stops in her tracks. Eve breathes deeply and stares at Sister Elisabeth. Falling to her knees, Sister Elisabeth begs, "Forgive me."

"I fucking dare you! Try and take my daughter one more time and I will destroy you and have your soul begging for mercy. Do you understand?" Eve bellows.

Looking up, Sister Elisabeth says nothing.

Grabbing her by the face, Eve continues, "Are you deaf? I said if you try and take my daughter from me one more time, or actually from anyone, I will destroy you and have your soul begging for mercy. Do you understand?"

"Yes."

Releasing her face, Eve stares at Sister Elisabeth. "Now leave my room."

Sister Elisabeth surrenders and leaves the room.

Baby Honey is sobbing her little heart out as she lies in her mummy's arms.

Transitioning back into her human form, Eve desperately tries to console her daughter, "Oh shh, shh, shh, shh, shh. I'm so sorry, Honey. Mummy's so sorry." Bringing her up to her face, Eve squeezes her daughter tight. "Mummy promises she won't do that again. The naughty lady was trying to take you from me – oh my baby, I'm so sorry. Please don't cry."

Now crying herself, Eve is devastated that she's scared her baby girl. Placing baby Honey down on the bed, Eve grabs her dressing gown and puts it on. She then wraps baby Honey in a blanket and decides to look for Lewis.

Eve steps out of her room into the gloomy corridor, lit only by dim candlelight. She hears the jingling of keys and doesn't know whether she should run back inside her room or continue towards the sound. Baby Honey starts to squirm inside her blanket. A light appears in the distance and the sound from the keys gets louder.

"Eve – is that you?"

"Yes."

Sister Marie appears from the darkness with a candle in her hand and smiles at Eve.

"Darling, what are you doing out in the corridor at night?"

"Erm, Honey wouldn't—"

"Oh my goodness," Sister Marie interrupts. "Is this your baby? We heard she'd arrived but were told that you were too sick for visitors."

"Yes, that's right. I'd lost a lot of blood during the birth and I wasn't able to walk for a little while. I had passed out and wasn't able to fully deliver her right away. It was touch and go for a little while. In the end, Sister Jesselle had to physically remove her from me."

"What a traumatising experience," Sister Marie says, appearing extremely concerned, "You have both been part of our prayer service every day since you went into labour."

"Thank you, Sister Marie."

"Aww, can I have a look at her?"

"Of course," Eve says as she pulls the blanket away from Honey's face.

"Oh my, you must be mighty proud. She's beautiful."

"Yes. I'm sorry, you're right. I shouldn't be wandering the corridors. I'm going to take her back to bed."

"Look, why don't you come with me, we'll get her some warm milk and some clean blankets." Placing her arm around Eve, Sister

Marie continues, "It's scary being a new mum. Don't worry, we're all here to help you. We are all chosen sisters of the Lord himself for a reason."

Eve hesitates, unsure whether she should follow Sister Marie.

"It's okay."

"But Sister Jesselle doesn't know I'm…"

"Oh don't worry about Sister Jesselle. She'll be fine."

"I was just looking for Lewis. He went with Sister Jesselle before and I wanted him to stay with me and Honey."

"Oh but Eve that is not permitted in the Lord's house. You mustn't lie with one another. Your child has been born out of wedlock. This is highly frowned upon. You must be married and declare your marriage by taking your vows before the Lord."

"Me and Lewis, get married?"

"Yes. You share a child. This child, in the eyes of the Lord, is a bastard. This child has been born out of wedlock. We do not judge here at the home. But I would highly recommend you consider the possibility of getting married here at the chapel. We could also welcome this one into the world officially by blessing her at the same time."

"I've never thought about it. But, well, yes, I suppose you're right."

"I can perform the ceremony for you. We can unite you all as one. Here we thrive from love. Our place of worship." She reaches out and grazes her fingertips across the grey stone. "These walls were built on love. Okay, so it would seem sometimes that love has been lost here, but I assure you, Eve, that is not the case. From love, we thrive. Your love for Lewis and your daughter has you thriving."

Honey holds Eve's finger with all her tiny fingertips. Gently kissing them, Eve smiles from ear to ear. Her heart is warm, but her head hangs heavy.

"My precious darling girl, I've seen that smile before. That smile you are wearing can only belong to someone who is smitten with love. Someone who is loved and who loves. Only those people are blessed with such beauty."

"If I agree to this, will you keep it a secret?"

"Why would you not wish to share your big day? I mean, the nunnery could use such an occasion to—"

"No!" Eve buts in. "You must not tell anyone, Sister Marie."

"Why, my child?"

"Just trust me on this, please."

Reaching out and touching Eve on the shoulder, Sister Marie replies, "Of course, my child. Please don't worry. If that is your wish, then I will tell nobody."

"Honestly, I need your word. I need you to promise me that you won't say anything to anyone. I need you to swear to your God that you will keep this between us unless I instruct otherwise. Sister Jesselle cannot find out about this. Please, Sister Marie, you have to promise me."

"My child, I promise. I won't breathe a word."

Eve begins to shake.

Sister Marie holds her tightly in her arms, "We can sort this for you and you can be one. My child, you are not alone."

Smiling as she looks to her daughter, Eve whispers, "Would you like that, baby girl? Mummy and daddy get married? And you get protection from Sister Marie's father?" Baby Honey squirms in her blanket, making baby grunting noises. Smiling from ear to ear once more, Eve says, "I'm going to take that as a yes."

"Come, let's go and get this little one some warm milk and extra blankets. What do you say, Honey?"

"I think she'd like that."

"I do, too. And Eve, I promise here we take your secrets to our grave."

Feeling safe, Eve says nothing as she follows Sister Marie down the corridor.

CHAPTER 12

Revenge

Two days have passed since Matthew met with Sandra. Standing in the dining room at his home, Matthew's scratching his head.

"What could these possibly mean?" Matthew says, confused.

"Mate, you've been looking at those doodles for ages now. Seriously, come get some food down ya. You're always lecturing me about eating."

"Phil, seriously, how can you eat at a time like this?"

"Are you kidding me? We almost got killed. I don't know about you, but I'm enjoying every single thing there is whilst I still can – that includes food and minus the alcohol of course."

Shaking his head, Matthew looks away from Phil, who is chowing down on BBQ ribs like they're going out of fashion. He's surrounded by masses of drawings, the ones Sandra threw at him before he left the room. Each crumpled up piece of paper contains its own unique drawing. Although, they all have something in common. On every sheet there's a small silver heart drawn in the centre of the paper. Holding one up, Matthew stares at what looks like some sort of forest. Looking closer, he sees a black bird in one of the trees. A tiny black stick figure stands alone in the forest. Matthew has no idea what this means. Picking up the next drawing, Matthew sees a chapel. The chapel is huge. Placed in the centre of the chapel is a basket. Inside the basket there appears to be a baby. Making his way across to the table with his sticky rib in hand, Phil picks up one of the sheets of paper and smears rib sauce on the corner of it, "So, what this about, then?" he says, his mouth full of food.

"Phil – you're getting sauce all over it. Pass it here."

Looking at the picture Phil's chosen, Matthew sees something disturbing. He peers closer at the image. His eyes tell no lies. In this image, surrounded by woodland, he sees two gravestones. Two silver hearts and two very clear names: 'Here lies Lauren Honey' and 'Here lies Evelyn Jade Honey'. Underneath where it says 'Evelyn Jade Honey', the words 'she is not yours to keep' have been written. Screwing this up, Matthew immediately charges to the bin and throws the picture inside it.

"Matthew, what's wrong, mate?"

Saying nothing, Matthew grabs a cigarette, lights it and heads towards the front door.

"Mate, I'm sorry. What did I say?" Phil calls after him.

Saying nothing still, Matthew opens the front door and slams it behind him.

Matthew marches down the street, smoking his cigarette so fast that the nicotine hits his brain in a rush. Keeping his head down, he has no clue where he's going. The only thing he does know is that he's one hundred percent not in the mood to be around people right now. At the end of Matthew's street there is an entrance that has two pathways. One continues as a stone path across the top of the beachfront and the other is made up with sand and leads onto the beach. Seeing as the tide is currently in as it's late, Matthew stays on the stone pathway. The path has benches and shelters sporadically placed along it. Lights are flickering from the lampposts. Some of the lampposts are dark as their bulbs have not been replaced, leaving certain sections of the pathway too dimly lit. Trying desperately to calm himself, Matthew breathes deeply. As he's inhaling he can taste the saltiness from the sea in the air. He hears the sound of the waves as they gently flow back and forth, and his frustration begins to subside. Taking in another deep breath, he suddenly feels as though he's being followed. Matthew turns. No one is there. Continuing to walk a few more feet again he feels someone in his presence but this time, he feels them standing behind him. But again, as he turns, he sees there's no one there. As Matthew reaches the end of the pathway, he feels a blow to the back of his legs. He falls to the floor, pain surging through the backs of his knees.

"Not so tough now, are ya?"

Matthew feels another blow to his legs. He turns and sees none other than Chief Inspector Lamont hovering over him, wearing a black sweatsuit and with a hood hanging heavy over his head. Clearly drunk, Lamont is brandishing a baseball bat. Matthew dodges the next swing, suddenly feeling empowered by the hate that he has for this man. Bouncing up off the ground Matthew shouts, "Come on then… you 'ave no fuckin' idea how long I've been waiting for this moment. Fuckin' bring it, you daft bastard."

There is no way Matthew is missing out on having his moment with this bully. Swinging once more, Lamont stumbles and misses his target.

"You think you can ruin me and get away with it, do ya?"

Swinging a further time, Lamont spins on his feet. He stops and puts his hand to his eyes, wobbling a bit. Seizing the moment, Matthew reaches out and rips the baseball bat from his enemy's hands. Lamont falls to the ground, "Go on then, fucking hit me with it, you fucking pussy!" He shouts. When Matthew doesn't move he shouts once more, "Yeah, fucking thought not, you fucking pussy. Couldn't save your daughter, couldn't save your wife and now you're just gonna—"

But before he can finish his sentence, Matthew smacks the baseball bat right across his head with a resounding crack. Lamont lies flat out on the floor. Matthew throws his coat over his head and runs back the way he just came with the baseball bat held tightly in his hand. He stops at the end of the pathway, out of breath. In a panic, he gets out his phone and rings Phil.

"Phil, please, I need your help."

"Matthew, what's wrong? Where are you?"

"I'm down by the pathway at the beach."

"What are you doing there?"

"I haven't got time to explain. Please, just come quickly."

"Mate, seriously calm down. You're going to have a heart attack or summit. I'm on my way, just stay there."

"Phil."

"Yeah?"

"Please be quick we haven't got a lot of time."

"I promise mate. I'm leaving now, I'll be as fast as I can."

"Thank you. Call me when you're near. And Phil…"

"Yeah?"

"Cover up."

Asking no more questions, Phil simply replies, "Will do, mate."

Waiting in anticipation, Matthew is pacing the same spot. He's panicking and doesn't know what to do. One of the voices in his head begins taunting him.

Gone and done it now, aven't ya? Good luck getting out of this one. Now you are a murderer.

Anxiety is surging throughout his body. Wanting to shut the voice up, Matthew shouts, "Be quiet! It was self-defence," as he smacks himself in the head.

Matthew, don't worry, a distant voice whispers.
We'll just throw the body in the sea. We'll get rid of it. No one will ever connect this to you. We can do this.

Looking up, Matthew's relived to see Phil approaching from out of the distance. Matthew runs towards him.

"Quick, come here."

"Are you okay, mate? Where'd you get that baseball bat from? Actually, why have you even got a baseball-bat?"

"Just shh and follow me."

Matthew drags him down the dark walkway, arriving back at the spot where he left Lamont's prone body. But there is no sign of him.

"What the…?" He scratches his head and points to the grass. "He was just here!"

"Who?"

"Duck!" Matthew yells.

Lamont has appeared from behind one of the sheltered seating areas and is charging straight for Phil. Panicked, Phil runs towards Matthew and positions himself directly behind him. Lamont is now just two meters away from the pair. Without hesitation, Matthew swings the bat. Lamont moves out of the way and Matthew misses. The pair are now in a standoff.

"Matthew, what the fuck? Where'd he come from?"

"Come on, Matthew, put the bat down, me and you have a one on one," Lamont says.

"Fine, have it your way," Matthew responds, throwing the bat to Phil. "But don't say I didn't warn you all those months ago."

"Oh, believe me, I'm going to enjoy this."

Lamont throws a punch, connecting with Matthew's face. Feeling the pain from the blow, Matthew stumbles slightly. His lip instantly fattens and blood travels down his chin.

"That was your one shot. Enjoy it."

Charging at Lamont, Matthew tackles him to the ground. The pair wrestle, throwing blow after blow at one another. Suddenly Lamont overpowers Matthew and throws him flat on his back. With Lamont on top of his body, Matthew struggles against his weight to get him off, hitting out with his fists.

"Matthew, he's got a knife!" Phil shouts.

Lamont pulls a blade from nowhere and attempts to stab Matthew in the throat. Phil shouts a warning and Matthew manages to grab Lamont's arm before the knife reaches his neck. He can feel Lamont's power as he desperately tries to push the blade into his neck. Matthew's hands are trembling. He isn't sure he's going to be able to hold Lamont's arm much longer. Looking up at Lamont, Matthew sees that blood is gushing down his face and his eyes are dark and filled with hate. This man is really trying to kill him. Giving it all his might, Matthew continues to hold Lamont's arm away from his neck but he's really growing weaker with every second that passes. Out the corner of his eye, Matthew sees Phil approach with the baseball bat in his hand. Phil swings and hits Lamont straight in the head.

"Get the fuck off my friend!" Phil shouts.

As Lamont falls, Matthew instantly jumps up, and disarms Lamont. Now in possession of the knife, Matthew sees red. This man was truly trying to kill him. He swings the knife and stabs Lamont in the top of his thigh. He twists the blade, then pulls it out. Screaming in pain, Lamont rolls around on the floor.

"Let that be a lesson to you. The next time you try and hunt me down like that – I will fucking kill you."

Phil swings the baseball bat once more and this time hits Lamont in his stab wound, "That's for trying to kill my friend, you piece of shit," he says.

As Matthew and Phil turn to leave, Lamont says, "I've not finished with you yet. You may have won this round, Honey, but next time you won't be so lucky."

CHAPTER 13

Night Terrors

Brennan is lost and confused in the depths of Moycullen Forest, struggling with a backpack that's almost equal in size to him. The middle-aged American paranormal activity hunter stands with a map and a compass in one hand and a torch in the other. It's a dark Wednesday evening in the middle of April and thankfully it's not too cold. Turning in the same spot, desperately trying to find his bearings, he once again consults his map and then decides to head north. He has thick mud smeared all over his clothes, but this determined individual is not giving up. He's on to something big and he knows it. Using all his might he strides on through the forest, until his feet suddenly begin sinking into the ground. The mud rises quickly, traveling past his shins. Thinking fast, he grabs a branch hanging from the tree next to him and uses it to pull himself out of the mud sink hole. Slightly out of breath, he says, "You weren't lying, were you, Tommy? Phffft, this is well and truly the fucking forest of horrors, man."

While cleaning himself off, suddenly he notices the ground before him has gone misty. He can no longer see his feet. Pushing his thick-framed glasses back up the bridge of his nose, he focuses his sight ahead of him. Once again consulting his map, he says, "Okay – you best hurry your ass up, man, or you're going to get stuck in this God forsaken forest all night."

Feeling as if he's no longer alone, he peers over his map, "Hello?"

No one answers, and he folds his map up and places it under his arm. Reaching inside his pocket, he pulls out his portable recording device and hits the record button.

"This is what you've come for," the thrill seeker tells himself, smiling from ear to ear. He places his mouth close to the speaker and begins talking, "So, I'm currently in Moycullen Forest, it's way into the night and guess what? Yeah, I'm lost. But you're not going to fucking believe this – crazy shit is already happening. Dudes, I'm fucking being surrounded by a thick mist. That can only mean one thing: the paranormal is coming."

Becoming more and more excited by the second, he follows the trail of the mist. Not only does he have the darkness of the night to contend with, as well as the mud that is continually trying to suck his feet underground, he's now unable to see his surroundings. He removes his glasses and wipes the lenses on the sleeves of his fleece. As he puts them back on, he sees what appears to be a female figure in the distance. Wasting no time, he shouts, "Excuse me, ma'am, can you tell me the way to the Moycullen Nunnery?"

Getting no response, he clambers over the tree stumps and twigs as he strives to make his way through the mist in the direction of the female.

"Ma'am, excuse me, I'm lost, can you point me in the direction of the nunnery?"

Suddenly the female goes out of sight. With his supernatural senses on high alert, this adrenaline fuelled, paranormal activity junkie is hyped!

"I swear this forest is the creepiest fucking forest. You guys, I'm so pumped right now."

Brennan thinks back to when he first heard about this nunnery and its wicked ways, from a drunk Irish man Tommy. It was two months ago in one of the Irish bars next to his office in New York City…

"So young Brennan, I hear you enjoy hunting the supernatural."
"Dude, I don't enjoy it – I fuckin' love it."

Laughing at his over the top response, Tommy replies, "Well young Brennan in that case I've got a place that will haunt you for years."

Sitting up in his seat Brennan replies, "You've got my attention. I'm listening."

"It has been deemed the most unholy place throughout the whole of Ireland. It is said that those who have journeyed to this poisoned land have never returned. Never seen again. In recent years, the younger ones, you know the ones that like to do those videos for the internet, them little fuckers, well they've ventured into the forest to test the stories – believe me when I say young Brennan, those young ones have never been seen again. I wouldn't say their death was worth the momentary attention and fame they were after but hey ho, the young ones of today will just never learn."

"Really, holy shit. This place sounds right up my street. Tommy, dude, you have to tell me where it is."

"The spirit world is not to be messed with young Brennan. It should be respected not tested. Do you understand what I mean by that?"

"Yes – Tommy I promise I'll respect it. Believe me, my mission for the paranormal is beyond wanting to create videos, and momentary fame. Please, you have to believe me, I have a bigger purpose than such vanity. Dude I'm doing this for something much greater than me. Something I need answers to that this universe cannot give me."

"Okay, so you think you're brave enough and have a great purpose to take on the most unholy of forests where so many have died?"

"You know what Tommy – yes, I am. Now come on, tell me where the forest is…"

"All in good time young Brennan."

Tapping his glass which is nearly empty, Tommy looks to Brennan.

Taking the hint, Brennan shouts, "Can we get another round, Tammy?"

"Sure one sec."

"Why thank you young Brennan. Now what is it you wanted to know?"

"Everything."

"Okay – I'll tell you everything I know. This forest will eat you alive. It's the most haunted location in Ireland. Many, many, many, many years ago this was sacred and holy ground. It houses one of the biggest,

most elegant and stunning chapels. Across the way from the chapel was a nunnery. The Moycullen Nunnery. A home for the unloved. A home for the ones who were supposed to be protected by their loved ones. A home for the ones who were forgotten. A home for the vulnerable souls deemed not wanted and unlovable. A home for lost girls and boys just like me."

"What?! Oh shit – I'm sorry Tommy I didn't know you were raised in an orphanage."

"Don't mither about that. I did okay." Laughing as he recalls the memories, "Oh some of those nuns though. If they loved you, they took you under their fucking wing. You were well and truly looked after and loved whole heartedly. But mark my words – if you got on the wrong side of one of those nuns, forget it, they'd fucking beat ya senseless. They didn't give a flying fuck, they'd be whipping the back of you until your skin would be raw and you'd be bleeding."

Mortified, Brennan says, "They can't do that!"

Laughing, he replies, "Why who was going to stop them? Remember, we're the unloved and no one was about to come to our rescue. Well, not during those times anyway. They didn't have anyone to answer to and so they wouldn't hesitate to beat the sins out of you."

"Oh shit that's terrible."

"Well, over the years the word got out about what the nuns were doing and so the residents of the surrounding villages didn't take too kindly to the cruel goings-on just down the way. Determined to put an end to the child cruelty, they came up with a plan. They formed a group and called themselves The Pitchfork Crew. They wanted to shut down the nunnery and take all of us children. Unfortunately like most things, this didn't go as planned."

"What you mean?"

"Well the sisters believed they were doing no wrong. They believed they had the right to remove sins in whichever way they saw fit. So when the Pitchfork Crew arrived at the nunnery, the most evil member of the nunnery was ready and waiting for them."

"Evil?"

"Yes – this one you wouldn't wish to have seen in your lifetime. Just one mention of her name and your spine would shudder. If the other nuns threatened to call her, believe me, you'd instantly beg for mercy. A

cruel woman she was. Just talking about her now sends shivers down my spine. This one I'll never forget – her name, Sister Fiona." Shuddering once more, Tommy grabs his pint and throws the remainder of this to the back of his throat, "Sister Fiona went to the gates and from that point, all hell broke loose."

"Why, what happened?"

"I can't even begin to tell you but put it this way, the way she protected those gates all those years ago, it's been said that she still protects them the same way today – from beyond the grave!"

"Tommy – dude, you have to tell me how I can get there?"

"Oh I will young Brennan but you have to promise me that you will be careful."

"I promise. Tommy tell me, is the nunnery still active?"

"As far as I'm aware yes. They've been trying to have it shut down for years. It has never happened and as time has gone on, the Moycullen Forest has become more and more sinister. This is now well and truly the land of the unloved."

Brennan trips over his own feet and falls to the ground. He picks himself back up and bends back down, vigorously patting the ground in a panic. When he fell, he dropped his recording device. Brennan feels a thick, cold, sticky substance sliding over his hand. Believing it is simply mud squelching through his fingers, he wipes his hand on his clothing and once again pushes the frame of his glasses back up the bridge of his nose. Shining his torch, Brennan sees that the substance he'd put his hand in was in fact a thick pool of blood. He runs behind a tree and vomits.

As the retching stops, he sees the red flashing light on his recording device flickering at the side of him. He reaches out to grab it and is caught off guard when he hears a female voice whisper down his ear, "I wouldn't carry on, if I was you…"

Breathing heavily, Brennan slowly turns, his torch firmly grasped in both of his hands. His body is trembling. His nerves are beginning to get the better of him. He sees there's no one there. Suddenly, the sound of a female giggling hysterically resonates throughout his eardrums. Panicking and frozen to the spot, Brennan is unaware that he's being watched. Looking to the device in his hand, Brennan is thankful when he sees that the red light is still flashing.

"I really hope you recorded that. Dudes, I'm not going to lie to you, I'm actually really fucking. Scared. Right. Now. I have lost all sense of direction and I have no fucking clue where I am. My legs have gone stiff but I'm not going to let this stop me, dudes. We're in this together."

Slowly making his way in a straight line as best he can, Brennan looks up and sees a huge glow set way back into the forest. No sooner has he taken his first step towards the direction of the light than the taunting female's voice sounds again, "You shouldn't be here."

Feeling brave, Brennan decides to speak out, "Why?" Hearing nothing, he again shouts, "Ma'am! Maybe you can help me?"

That's when a human body drops from the tree branch in front of him.

Laughing, the female voice returns, "Help you? I cannot help you. You see, I cannot help you because I am dead."

The menacing laughter resumes as Brennan looks in horror at the pregnant woman with the rope around her neck. Vomit surges into his mouth and he leans forward and throws up again. He wipes his mouth and whispers to himself, "Come on, get a grip, Brennan, don't let this forest beat you. It's all in your head."

"I told you – you shouldn't be here," the echoing voice says.

Wiping the excess vomit from around his mouth, Brennan shouts, "Wait, was that you?"

There is no response.

"Who did that to you?" he shouts.

As the silence becomes deadly, Brennan spits the remaining bits of vomit in his mouth on the ground and repeats to himself, "It's all in your head. Just keep going. Just get to the nunnery and you'll be fine. Remember, fear is a good thing, fear is your mind's way of telling you you're onto something big. We never stop at the terror barrier. We smash through it."

With his mini pep talk over, Brennan makes his way through the trees. Shining his torch, he sees a grey bricked pathway just ahead of him. Desperate to get onto the path, Brennan begins to run.

The branches grab at his arms and legs and face, as if in a desperate attempt to keep him inside the darkest depths of the forest. Fighting back, Brennan slowly drags himself on to the pathway. He lies on the cold stone ground, breathing heavily. He's cold, dirty and has an acid taste burning at the back his throat. With his arms flat out, Brennan's in shock. Adrenaline is surging throughout his body.

"Come on, we're almost there. Almost at the finish line, dude. Come on, get up."

Brennan is determined. He's not going to let this forest stop him from reaching that nunnery. Dragging himself up off the ground, he heads towards the light.

Following him, the deceitful mist circulates on the ground, getting thicker. Like an elegant dance, the mist intertwines with itself. It travels through Brennan's nostrils and down his throat, making him choke. The powerful and unknown element suddenly drains the oxygen from Brennan's body and rapidly takes his breath away. Falling to the ground once more, Brennan gasps for air. On his knees, he glances up. In a daze, he sees the female figure glide between two trees.

"Help me. Please."

There is no response. Brennan is aware he could die at any precious moment, and though he is desperate to find out who she is, he is equally desperate to breathe again. Coughing, he collapses onto his back. Drifting in and out of consciousness, he whispers, "Please, who are you…?"

Taunting him, she says, "You did that to me." Appearing behind Brennan she gently whispers into his ear, "Do you not recognise me?"

Slowly turning his head, Brennan sees there's no one there.

"Come on, Brennan, please get up. Please – you can do this. Come on, you're almost there," he tells himself.

Brennan drags his limp body up off the ground. As he takes his fourth step, he trips over a stone and falls, landing back on the cold ground. He slides his back up against the nearest tree. As if sensing an opportunity, the mist instantly surrounds Brennan. Gaining power, it begins to thicken. In fact, the mist is now so thick, Brennan's no longer able to see what's in front of him. With his torch in his hand,

Brennan turns the switch to its maximum capacity, although this doesn't appear to make any difference as the mist is far too dominant. Throwing his head back and closing his eyes, Brennan is just about to accept defeat when suddenly he sees Tommy's face appear in his mind.

"This is serious, young Brennan. No matter what, no matter how weak you become, you must never give in to the Forest. Never surrender your soul to the Forest. I promise you this, young Brennan, your body will be eaten whilst you live, and your soul will remain a victim to the Forest for all eternity."

Brennan is confused and unsure of what to do next. As much as he loves the supernatural world, he has allowed his mind to become weakened and is rapidly deteriorating. Not only this, he's seriously freaked out. Fear is no longer being a motivational friend and is in fact taking over his mind. All Brennan wants to do is quit but he's certain that the words Tommy spoke are true. He knows he must get back up and fight against the forces surrounding him. Dragging himself up using the support of the tree, he pushes the glasses back up the bridge of his nose. Brennan's exhausted, scared and has never felt so alone in all his life, but he's determined to reach the nunnery. He has been in many fucked up situations before, but Brennan's never experienced anything quite like this. His mind begins racing, desperately trying to work out how he can free himself from this trap.

Biting his bottom lip, he is breathing in deeply and praying for the nightmare he's stuck inside to be over. As he exhales, Brennan gains a slight amount of strength. Determined not to die, he bravely attempts to shout for answers, "What..." He trails off and coughs. Catching his breath, he tries again, "What do you..." But again, his vocal cords aren't quite ready. Coughing and clearing his throat once more, this time he shouts, "What do you mean?" He continues, "Tell me who you are, please. I want to help you."

"Riddles in the night," the female voice says. "You see – I'm not where you last saw me. But what I can tell you is that I like to play in the spot where I last was..."

Insane female laughter takes over the forest, echoing through the trees. Attempting to work out what these words could possibly mean, Brennan again feels a huge presence behind him. Slowly turning, he sees the swinging female corpse has returned and she's dangling from the same tree.

Brennan's first instinct is to drag his limp body and run as far away from the female corpse as possible. But there's one thing stopping him – his curiosity. Instead of running, Brennan decides to make his way towards the swinging corpse. With every step he takes, his heart is beating erratically. With every step he takes, his breathing is becoming out of sync. And with every step he takes, his imagination is playing tricks on him! Briefly glancing to his hand to check that his recording device is still switched on, as he looks back up, Brennan sees the swinging corpse is no longer there.

"You shouldn't be here, Brennan."

"Wait – how do you know..."

"Your name..."

"Seriously, who are you?"

A sudden ice-cold breeze travels down Brennan's neck. Feeling a strong presence behind him, he bravely turns. Yelping out loud, Brennan sees the female corpse flash in front of his face. Stumbling back, Brennan is horrified as he sees her clearly. His eyes tell no lies! She's standing directly in front of him and this woman's appearance is sickening. Her complexion is deep grey. Her eyes have dark rings around them. She has a deep laceration in her throat that oozes blood. Wearing a white gown that's stained with bright red blood down the lower half, this woman is no longer pregnant. Lying inside her arms is the corpse of a baby. A small, grey, decaying baby covered in blood.

"Don't you remember, Brennan? This is our baby." Tilting her head and stroking the baby's face, she continues, "Don't you remember us, Brennan?"

Brennan's jaw drops. He doesn't say a single word.

Not giving up, she continues, "You promised you'd be ours forever." Taking one step closer and looking down at her dead baby, she says, "Love us forever, you said. Love us for all eternity, you said. Why are you just standing there? I thought you'd be happy to see us.

I thought you'd be happy to meet your son. *Brennan* – what's wrong with you?" Becoming angry, she shouts, "Brennan, speak to me! Why do you look like you've seen a ghost. *Brennan* – what's wrong with you?"

Brennan sheds a single tear. "Janine?"

No sooner has he whispered her name than she disappears.

His sight goes hazy and his head begins to spin. Losing his balance, Brennan falls to the ground, dropping his torch and his recording device. Fliting in and out of consciousness, Brennan suddenly sees the female flash before his eyes. She's laughing hysterically and says, "Your turn, daddy."

Almost instantly, Brennan's out cold on the ground and the mist begins coating his body.

Sweating from head to toe, Brennan gasps for air and throws himself forward. He pats himself down; much to his relief, he's alive and in one piece, though he realises he's wearing clothes that are not his own. He has no clue where he is or how he got there. At the side of the bed that he's lying in is a small wooden table. Resting on this are his glasses. He puts them on and glances around the room. Inside the room is a wicker built rocking chair on which sits his backpack. The walls are extremely high and made of grey stone. As Brennan looks to his right, he sees a huge rounded wooden door with a black doorknob. The room has a medieval theme throughout and is dark, dingy and extremely unwelcoming. There is a tiny beam of natural daylight radiating through the small window positioned up high – a window that is too high to reach and way too small to fit through.

Brennan clambers his way out of the thick grey woollen sheets. Unsteady on his feet, he stumbles across the room to retrieve his backpack. Opening it, he panics. His recording device isn't there. He frantically pulls out all the items inside the backpack and throws them onto the chair, but his recording device is still nowhere to be seen. Brennan drops to his knees and begins searching the ground. Looking under the bed, he sees nothing but dust balls and what appears to be animal hairs. Hearing the jingling of keys coming from the hallway, Brennan quickly jumps up off the ground, dusts himself down and rushes back to the rocking chair. He shoves all his belongings back inside the backpack and throws it back where it was, then leaps into bed and wraps himself inside the bedsheets.

With a *click* and *thud*, the door slowly creaks open. Brennan peeps through the slight gap in his eyes and sees a nun peering her head inside the room. Closing the door behind her, she makes her way across the room, opens his backpack and begins rummaging inside.

"Erm, excuse me, ma'am, I don't think that's very holy of you now, is it?"

Jumping, the Sister throws the backpack back onto the chair and turns, "Oh, I'm sorry. I thought you were sleeping. I was trying to see if you maybe had any identification on you, that's all."

"That's fine, ma'am. I won't tell on you, but only if you tell me where I am."

"It's actually Sister Alannah, and not ma'am, if you please. Yes, of course I can tell you. You're currently at my home, the Moycullen Nunnery."

"What?!" Whispering to himself he says, "Holy shit, I made it. Ha."

"Sorry, what did you just say?"

"Oh, nothing. Sister Alannah, do you know how I got here?"

"Yes – you were found at the gates two days ago. You were unconscious. Our Mother Superior, Sister Kathryn found you. She called for me and then we carried you in here as you seemed very unwell." Making her way to his bedside, Sister Alannah continues, "Your clothes were filthy and had what looked like blood all over them. I got you some fresh clothing, cleaned your glasses and then placed you in bed."

"That's very kind of you, Sister Alannah. Thank you." Scratching his head in disbelief, Brennan whispers, "Man, Tommy was right, this forest is freakin' awesome."

"Sorry, who is Tommy?"

Laughing to himself he says, "Don't worry about it."

Smiling she says, "So you're American?"

"Yes, ma'am. I mean – Sister Alannah."

"What part of America are you from?"

"I'm from the big apple. NYC – New York City."

Her eyes widen as she replies, "Wow, I've always wanted to go there."

"Well, why don't you sometime?"

"I can't." Looking sad, she continues, "I have to stay within these walls. I have promised my life to Our Father. My path has been chosen for me and I cannot leave."

"Wow, so this is quite a serious commitment you make then, huh?"

"Oh, yes. Of course, he is our saviour. He sacrificed everything for us and we owe him the same."

"So, Sister Alannah – you have no clue how I got to the gates?"

"No. I'm sorry."

"It's okay. Erm – did I happen to have any, like, devices with me?"

"What do you mean?"

"Did I have anything in my hands when you brought me in?"

"No – not that I can remember. Just the backpack placed at the side of you."

"Damn it."

"Why, did you have something important?"

"I can't find my recording device."

"Your what…?"

"My recording device. It's okay – I'm sure I'll come across it when I go back into the forest."

"Wait – go back?"

"Yeah."

"You can't – you mustn't."

"Why not?"

"The forest is not to be played around with. Your safety is here inside the nunnery. You don't know the forest. You can't just go wandering around."

"But you know the forest, right…?"

"Yes."

"Well, it's simple. You can take me, then."

Appearing slightly uncomfortable, Sister Alannah heads towards the door and says, "Erm – I'll go fetch your clothes for you. I'll be right back. We are about to have lunch so maybe once you are dressed I could take you to the hall and get you some food? You must be hungry by now – you've not eaten for two days."

Deciding not to ask the question again about going back into the forest, due to her reaction, Brennan simply replies, "Sure. That would be great. Thank you very much, Sister Alannah."

As she reaches for the doorknob, Sister Alannah turns and says, "What's your name by the way?"

"My name's Brennan."

"Nice to meet you, Brennan from New York."

"Nice to meet you too, Sister Alannah from the forest."

Smiling, Sister Alannah leaves the room and closes the door behind her.

CHAPTER 14

Almost...

At the Moycullen Nunnery, meals take place in the huge dining room. Standing strong and in perfect symmetry are seven dark wooden dining tables. On either side of the tables are eight wooden stools, which appear both uncomfortable and uninviting. The tables are bare. At the rear of the room, centre stage, is a table that sits on a raised platform and has a tiny wooden staircase leading up to it on either side. This is the table for the sisters. Set with gold trimming, gold drinking goblets, gold placemats and gold cutlery, the sisters' table is pristine. Hanging from the ceiling and hovering above each of the tables are large metal chandeliers. These stunning vintage pieces each hold eighty pure white French candles. The candles are only lit during special occasions that celebrate the worshiping of the Lord himself, their Father.

Sister Jesselle marches through the hall, her shoulders back and her nose in the air. Each step she takes can be heard echoing throughout. She takes her position at the rear of the hall up high on the platform centre stage so that she can oversee everything. She stands there proudly with her head raised. She is then closely followed by a group of her fellow sisters who each climb the staircase which is the closest to their seat and stand next to their designated places, the Sisters then await the arrival of the children.

Looking to Sister Marie, Sister Jennifer says, "Where's Sister Alannah?"

"I have no clue," Sister Marie replies, shrugging her shoulders.

The children enter the hall in two perfect lines. The girls form one line and the boys form another. The girls are wearing grey woollen chequered dresses with black collars, grey woollen knee-high socks and worn black matt shoes. Their hair is scraped back and tied tightly into a bun; not so much as a strand sits out of place. The boys are wearing long-sleeved grey shirts with black ties, grey woollen vests, grey woollen shorts that travel just past the knee, grey socks and worn black matt shoes. They all have the same hairstyle, which is short on the sides and slightly longer on the top. The children all look immaculate. Without saying a single word, they stand at the table behind their designated seats.

The silence is unnerving. Amongst the youngsters are Freddie, Terence and Rupert. Lewis is also present and is positioned at the front of the hall. Baby Hope is sound asleep in her big brother's arms. Lewis rocks her back and forth.

"Find her," Sister Jesselle says, nodding at Sister Elisabeth.

Without saying a single word, Sister Elisabeth bows her head and leaves the hall. Her head still held high, Sister Jesselle watches as the children stand silently. She is embracing the power and the control she has over the room. Taking a step forward she says, "Bow your heads."

Without so much as a second thought, every person within the hall bows their head.

"Today's prayer will be of a different kind." Pausing for a moment, Sister Jesselle looks around the hall before continuing, "A different kind of worship. A—"

"Excuse me, Sister Jesselle," Sister Kathryn butts in, "but I think we should stick to our normal prayer. I know you are keen to help us here, but as Mother Superior I believe the children need stability and that prayer has been recited for hundreds of years, this goes against—"

"Did I not just tell you to bow your head?" Sister Jesselle barks.

"Yes, but—"

"I don't want to hear it. Bow your head, Sister. Today we are doing prayer my way."

Sister Kathryn looks around the hall, then bows her head.

"Now, where was I – that's it, today's worship is of a different kind." Sister Jesselle makes her way down the wooden staircase and heads to a table where some of the young girls are standing, her footsteps echoing around the hall. One child has caught her interest. She stops in front of Rita and cups her face in her hand, "Open your eyes, child," she whispers.

Rita immediately opens her eyes. Gazing deep into her eyes, Sister Jesselle sees a looming dark grey cloud. As the cloud descends, all that can be seen is a thick blanket of black. Curled into a ball at the bottom of the dark abyss is Rita's soul. This young girl is trapped. Content with her findings, Sister Jesselle smiles as she whispers, "That's a good girl. Now close your eyes." Making her way around the hall once more she announces, "Today we worship my universe." Prouder than ever, feeling powerful and ready to truly dominate the hall, Sister Jesselle bellows, "Each of you repeat after me – I give my existence."

In unison, the children and the Sisters say, "I give my existence."

"To powers much greater than I."

"To powers much greater than I."

"I surrender my life."

The children and sisters embrace the words spoken, their voices becoming deeper. Unbeknownst to them, they are slowly surrendering to the words being chanted.

"I surrender my life."

"I hand over my soul."

Now, their voices are gaining a deep, morbid, monotone vibration. They are unaware of the impact that this merciless chant is having upon them. Every word spoken absorbs a tiny molecule of their purity. Imprisoned within their own minds, they continue to repeat the sadistic words Sister Jesselle speaks.

"I hand over my soul."

Standing in the centre of the room, Sister Jesselle looks to the candles in the chandeliers. The pure white candles all turn black! She tilts her head and huge green flames gust from the candles. Feeling stronger than ever, Sister Jesselle shouts, "My fate has been chosen!"

As the children and sisters become one with the words and slowly submit themselves, their voices are no longer their own.

"My fate has been chosen."

Getting louder, Sister Jesselle shouts, "My path has been aligned."

"My path has been aligned."

Sister Jesselle notices that across the hall, young Oliver has opened his eyes. She rushes over to the young boy. Turning him around to face her, she kneels, her eyes glowing. Her smile extends across her face. Holding Oliver by the chin, she gazes at the beauty of her evil that is now lying within him. Her plan is coming together. Young Oliver's eyes are turning jet black. His skin tone is slowly changing to a shade of grey. Standing, Sister Jesselle continues, "I embrace the evil within me."

Once again in unison, they chant, "I embrace the evil within me."

Walking back up the staircase to the table where her fellow sisters stand, Sister Jesselle heads to the empty space where Sister Alannah should be sitting. She stares at Sister Jennifer. In a trance like state, Sister Jennifer is also absorbing the words. Peering down the table, Sister Jesselle sees that all the sisters are wearing the same expression. Looking out across the hall, content, she continues, "I am contained by the darkness upon me."

The temperature in the room becomes ice cold.

"I am contained by the darkness upon me."

No sooner have the words left Oliver's and Rita's mouths than the two children begin levitating. Rita's eyes shoot open. Like Oliver's, they are jet black and her skin is a deep sinister shade of grey. They are the mirror image of the evil that has intruded into their lives and captured their souls.

With her head low, Sister Jesselle scans the perimeter of the room. "I will sacrifice my body to allow my owner to reign," she continues.

At the back of the room, three of the young girls are now beginning to transform, just like Oliver and Rita. The children and nuns are all locked deep inside the impure chant, unable to break free. They continue to repeat Jesselle's words, "I will sacrifice my body to allow my owner to reign."

"I will submit to the…"

Suddenly one of the huge wooden doors creaks open. Knocked off track, Sister Jesselle storms towards the entrance into the hall to see what the commotion is. In a fluster, Sister Alannah scurries into the hall with Brennan trailing closely behind her. Sister Jesselle charges at Sister Alannah and drags her and their new guest out onto the corridor before they have chance to see what is taking place inside the hall.

"What do you think you're playing at? Who is this man? And why are you so late?" Sister Jesselle shouts.

"I'm sorry, Sister Jesselle," Sister Alannah mumbles.

"That doesn't answer my question now does it?"

"Sister Jesselle, please accept my apologies. You see, I was just helping Brennan to become acquainted with the premises."

"Brennan?"

"Yes. Did you not hear? Brennan is the young man whom Sister Kathryn and I found by the gates two nights ago. He's been unconscious until now."

"No – I didn't hear about this. Yet again you and Sister Kathryn are deciding to keep secrets. We will continue this discussion later." Looking Brennan up and down, Sister Jesselle peers back at Sister Alannah once more and says, "I suggest you and Sister Kathryn come to my chambers this evening and we can discuss matters further then." Putting out her hand she says, "Stay here while I check the hall. We were in the middle of a very important prayer."

Sister Jesselle enters the hall and whispers, *"Ti rilascio per ora."*

Instantly, Oliver and Rita return to the ground. All the children and sisters lower their heads as their skin tone gradually resumes its natural shade.

Content with the transition, Sister Jesselle heads out of the hall and back into the corridor, "Be quiet when you enter the hall," she says, looking to Sister Alannah and her guest. "As I said, we are in the middle of a deep prayer. Any noise could be disturbing. Sister Alannah, take your usual place; and Brennan, you may sit at the front next to Lewis."

"Erm, that's great and all, ma'am, but who's Lewis?"

"Sister Alannah, you will show Brennan to his seat," Sister Jesselle says sternly.

They cautiously enter the hall. Sister Alannah forgets to close the door behind her. And so, as soon as they've entered the hall, the door slams with an almighty *bang*. It echoes through the hall, and the children and sisters begin coughing as they snap out of their trance. Shaking their heads, the sisters look at one another. They all have confused expressions upon their faces. They have no clue what has just happened.

Suddenly one of the little girls shouts, "Help! Renee is on the floor."

Turning, Sister Jesselle sees Renee convulsing on the ground. Rushing to her aid she shouts, "Sister Kathryn, go and get Mark from the kitchen immediately!"

A moment or so passes before Sister Kathryn rushes back from the kitchen with Mark in tow. Kneeling at the side of Renee, Mark sees she's no longer convulsing but she's very weak. Scooping up her tiny body, Mark carries her out of the hall. As the commotion slowly descends, the children and the sisters each take their seats

"Oh my, I'm so sorry," Sister Alannah says.

"Go and take your seat, Sister Alannah," Sister Jesselle shouts.

Being dragged to the front of the hall, by Sister Alannah, Brennan is seated at a table next to a young-looking man.

"Erm, you'll have to sit here, I hope you don't mind?"

"Sure – that's cool. Awesome, thank you so much Sister Alannah for your help."

Sister Alannah then runs up the staircase and stands next to Sister Jennifer.

Looking to Lewis, Brennan says, "Wow what a catch these nuns are, man. You must be in your element here, dude."

Not looking impressed, Lewis replies, "They are my superior sisters, what would I want with them?"

"Erm, yeah, sure." Feeling slightly awkward Brennan says, "Aw, is this your baby? Dude, she's cute."

"No, she is also my sister. My daughter is with her mother."

Feeling uncomfortable, Brennan decides it's best to stop speaking. Looking around the hall, he sees the sea of children all dressed in grey, they each have dark rims around their eyes and pale looking skin. Not one of them says a single word. Looking to Sister Alannah, Brennan shrugs his shoulders and mimes, "What's this?"

Whispering back, Sister Alannah says, "Please just shh."

Sister Jesselle rings the bell. Almost instantly the doors at the side of the staircases next to the top table fling open. Dressed head to toe in black, wheeling trolleys containing plates of food, are the nunnery's chefs and waiting staff, all of whom are male. As they begin placing the food in front on the children, suddenly the door creaks open once more.

Making her way into the hall is Eve. She's cradling her daughter. Marching at a rapid pace, Eve is heading to the top table. Following her into the hall is none other than Sister Elisabeth. Heading straight to Sister Jesselle, Sister Elisabeth whispers into her ear, nodding her head in approval. With her head low, Sister Elisabeth walks to the high-top table and seats herself.

Eve takes her seat next to Sister Marie who is seated on her left, "Can I have a word, please?" she says.

Sister Briana, an oversized sister who has a chubby face and rounded glasses perched on the bridge of her nose sat to the right of Eve, coos over the baby, "Oh, Sister Eve, is this the baby?"

"Yes, Sister Briana, please say hello to Honey."

"Oh, Sister Eve, she is just beautiful. Please can I hold her?"

"Sure."

Passing baby Honey to her fellow sister, Eve grabs Sister Marie by the arm and pulls her into the corner of the hall.

"What is wrong, my dear?" Sister Marie asks.

"Sister Marie, you were right, we must marry. Lewis and I must be wed. And Honey must be baptised immediately. Should anything happen to me, it is my desire that you, Sister Jennifer, Sister Cathleen and Sister Alannah take over the care and protection of Honey in my absence. You all have the combined qualities of the sisterhood that I have grown to admire and I believe each of these, when combined, will ensure Honey has the best start in life. You are strong and fearless. Sister Jennifer is the gentle giant. Sister Cathleen is highly educated. Sister Alannah is…"

Interrupting, Sister Marie says, "Sister Eve, my beautiful girl, calm down, nothing is going to happen to you. Please don't worry."

"You don't understand, this might be my only chance. Please will you wed us?"

"Of course, my dear."

"Great – tonight. You will marry us tonight. Just as the sun sets and the sky turns purple, you will connect us both as one and baptise Honey. My family will be whole."

"If this is your wish, then so be it, my child."

"It is, Sister."

"Then tonight it is."

"But, Sister, we cannot wed in the chapel."

"Huh, what do you mean?"

"I haven't got time to explain. Find somewhere else within the grounds to wed us."

"I…"

"Shh… she's watching us. Just think of somewhere, Sister. You know the grounds better than I do."

Eve glances over at Sister Jesselle and sees that she is staring intently at them. Eve bows her head and walks back to her seat, followed by Sister Marie. Eve then takes Honey from Sister Briana and walks along to the table where Lewis sits.

"Lewis, we must leave," she tells him. "I need to speak with you."

"Eve, we cannot leave. We have to stay in the hall."

"Lewis, please. Honey isn't well," Eve lies. "She needs us both."

"Really? Oh no, what's wrong with her?"

"I can't explain now, we need to leave."

Just then Brennan leans across and says, "Aww, dude, is this your baby? She's cute. Hey, little one."

Looking at him with a confused expression, Eve says, "Excuse me, but who are you?"

"I'm Brennan. I was found outside the gates."

"Okay, Brennan. Well do you mind? This is kind of a private conversation."

"Sure thing, consider me not here," he replies, looking sheepish.

Eve turns back to Lewis. "Come on," she says.

"What shall I do with Hope? I don't want her getting poorly too."

"Lewis, it's fine, just bring her. Honey isn't contagious."

Lewis gets up and the pair make their way out of the hall. But just as they start off down the corridor Eve hears, "Stop!"

The pair don't move. Looking to Lewis, Eve whispers, "Don't say a word."

Not only does Lewis not say a word, he doesn't so much as flinch.

Reaching the pair, Sister Jesselle says, "And where do you think you're going?"

"The girls are tired, Sister Jesselle. We thought we would put them down to rest. They were about to interrupt the peace of the hall. We didn't want to disturb the children."

"Is this right, Lewis?"

Again, not saying a word, Lewis simply nods his head.

"Okay, lay the children and I will collect you later." Sister Jesselle steps closer to Eve and takes her by the chin, "If you are lying to me, child, remember what I said – her soul for yours."

Dragging her chin out of Jesselle's hand, Eve says nothing and makes her way down the corridor.

"Don't let your human nature get you killed, Eve." Sister Jesselle yells as they leave.

They arrive in Eve's room and Eve closes the door behind them. Lewis places Hope inside Honey's cot and Eve places Honey in the centre of her bed between two pillows. Relieved to finally be alone with Lewis after her rather confusing morning, Eve goes to him and whispers, "Hold me – please."

Saying nothing, Lewis reaches out his arms and holds Eve.

Feeling safe, Eve says, "I could stay here for a lifetime."

"Eve, what's wrong?"

"Lewis, do you love me?"

"Yes – of course. Why would you even ask me that?"

"Because sometimes I feel that your fear for Sister Jesselle overtakes the love you hold for me."

"Fear?"

"Yes – fear. Put it this way, if Honey and I were being attacked by Sister Jesselle, would you save us?"

Laughing, he replies, "Eve, you know there would be no saving you. Now would I die with you both? Yes – of course, that goes without saying. I couldn't live my life without either one of you." Holding Eve by her shoulders he continues, "Where is this coming from?"

"Lewis, I fear my time is limited and I just want to be sure that Honey will be protected. I know this identity of being Eve will soon be lost. All we will know and see is the evil that I truly am. I really don't want Honey to go through this. I don't want her to know the truth. I don't want her to know that her mother is impure and evil. Please, Lewis, I don't want her seeing me this way."

"Babe…"

"No, Lewis, please listen to me. You don't understand. In fact, you can't understand, because part of you was once pure and you know it, you'll never forget the purity that still runs through you. You may have surrendered your soul to us but you still have your memory – I, on the other hand, do not. All that I am is evil. All that I know is evil. All that I have or should I say have had during my existence is Jezebel."

"Eve, what's this about?"

Ignoring Lewis, Eve continues, her thoughts spiralling, "And yet when Honey came along, my inner thoughts changed. The way my black heart beats changed. I get this overpowering surge of emotion.

A huge ball of love that I cannot contain. It travels all round my heart, mind and body. And no matter what, my inner evil cannot touch this – it cannot stop the surge of love once it has taken over. I feel somewhat – and I know this sounds ridiculous, but I feel as if I am solely human, not just an entity who can transform and adapt to being human. I feel this power within me and it is telling me that I was once like you were, a loved individual who had a true human form and a real family in this world."

"Awww, baby, don't worry, you're a new mum. Everything is going to seem confusing to you right now, especially in your human form, that's natural for mankind. I know these times are challenging. I went through it enough with my earth mother, Alice, when she had my brothers and my sister, maybe not Freddie so much but certainly the younger ones. She would get super emotional. It's just—"

"No, Lewis – you don't understand. I shouldn't feel like your earth mother. I'm an entity. I am not human."

"Eve, I don't know what you want me to say…"

"Lewis, I want Honey to remain pure." Looking at her daughter with tears in her eyes, Eve becomes frustrated. "Argh – but how can I want this?" Not giving Lewis the opportunity to answer, Eve continues with her rant, "Lewis, can't you see? It's not right. If I'm solely evil, why would I want our daughter to remain pure in a world where I know its fate? And the cost at which this will come?"

Eve walks towards Honey, who is peacefully sleeping on the bed. She closes her eyes and allows her tears to fall, "Our baby girl's options are to either remain pure in a world we know is impure, a world we know will not be this way for much longer, or to become something that I don't even want to bear thinking about as a mother. Our precious baby girl becoming a mirror reflection of the impure and sick evil that lies within us both." Eve wipes her face and clears the lump in her throat. "Really, are those our precious baby girl's only options?"

Lewis walks over to Eve and cradles her in his arms, "Shh, no babe, of course they're not."

"Lewis, stop trying to sugar coat this. Seriously, right now I feel as though you're not understanding a fucking word I'm saying.

Lewis, I honestly do not know who I am, I don't know how I got here. All I do know is that our baby girl is pure. She has no evil within her. Not from me and not from you. Can't you see, that's got to mean something..."

"What, Eve? What does it mean? Because I'm confused."

"Lewis, it clearly means that I'm pure, too."

"Huh... Eve, you know who your creator is."

"What is wrong with you? How can you not see what I am saying?" Pushing herself away from him Eve continues, "Lewis – look at the facts, it makes no logical sense. It is impossible for Honey to be pure if I am solely evil."

"Shhhh... Eve, please, you're going to make yourself ill," Lewis gently whispers.

Aware she's getting nowhere, Eve once again begins tearing up, but this time it's with anger. Nothing she is saying is making sense to Lewis, but it makes perfect sense to her. Desperate to try to get him to understand, Eve begs for answers as she gently sobs into Lewis's chest. She's so confused and is trying to work out the puzzle inside her head.

"I'm sorry," Eves says, the tears streaming down her face. "I just want to know who I am for her."

Saying nothing, the pair stand in the centre of the room in each other's arms. Trying to regain her composure, Eve goes over to the tiny sink in her room. As she turns on the tap, she looks at the state of her face in the mirror. Her skin is red and blotchy. Shaking her head, Eve splashes the cold water on her skin. Feeling brave, she blurts out what's really on her mind, "I think we should get married and have Honey baptised."

"What? You know Sister Jesselle will find out."

"Hear me out. I was speaking to Sister Marie earlier."

"Yeah, so? Eve, she'll kill us both."

"Lewis, please just stop for a minute." Pausing she looks at Lewis, he says nothing and so she continues, "I want Honey to remain pure and have protection. I also need you here with me and Honey. I need you in this room helping me. This is the only way, Lewis. Please, I really don't know what's going on with me right now but I know I can't do this anymore. I don't quite understand my existence. I'm confused and I'm seeing things. Lewis, I'm having nightmares."

"Nightmares? Like what?"

"They're not what you think."

"Well, tell me then."

"I can't, you really won't understand this."

"Eve, try me."

Eve takes a deep breath. She doesn't know whether she should tell Lewis. She looks up at him, desperately trying to gather the inner strength to speak. Fiddling with her fingers, Eve makes her way to her daughter on the bed and strokes her warm cheek.

"Eve – please, talk to me," Lewis says.

Turning, she says, "Lewis, that's the thing. I don't feel like I can anymore."

Lewis makes his way to her and holds her face. Saying nothing he kisses her on the lips. With her emotions high, a single tear rolls down Eve's cheek. Gazing into his eyes, Eve gets a sudden rush of love. Reaching out, Lewis removes Eve's veil and throws it onto the floor. He tucks her beautiful thick brown hair behind her ears and says, "There's the beautiful girl I fell in love with." Kissing her once more, Lewis runs his fingers through her hair. This instantly sends pleasurable tingles throughout her body. The pair are locked in the moment. Pressing his nose against hers, he gently kisses her lips.

"Eve – you can tell me anything. Please, speak to me. What's going on in that whirlwind mind of yours?"

Removing his hands from her face, Eve sits herself at the end of her bed. She decides to tell Lewis the truth, "The dreams I've been having…" Eve fidgets, not making eye contact with Lewis as she continues, "It's the same dream but each time I feel differently."

"Okay, go on."

"It's completely dark. There's nothing around me. There are no landmarks, no people, no streets, nothing! It's just black. You know like when we peer at the sky from this planet at night-time and it's a great big blanket of darkness? Well, it's the same as that – completely black. I'm running, and I'm running, and I'm running, and yet I'm getting nowhere. Then I get a chill down my spine and I suddenly feel an unwelcome presence behind me but I dare not turn around. I'm running with fear. Lewis, I'm running away from something but I don't know what it is. All I know is it feels like a trap."

Sitting next to her, Lewis says, "Okay, so that could mean…."

Interrupting him, Eve says, "Please, Lewis, let me finish."

"Sorry."

"I keep running. I'm trying to catch my breath and I can't. And even though I can hardly breathe, I just know I must keep going. I don't even attempt to turn around. I fear for my life. And so I just keep running, and running, and running, and I'm still getting nowhere. But you see, here's the thing: I'm not alone. I've got Honey in my arms. She wrapped in white sheets and she's pure. She's so beautiful and so pure. She's not tainted. Not even slightly."

"Right, but—"

"Lewis, please let me finish!" Eve barks, frustrated by his interruptions.

Lewis remains quiet.

"I look down at her as I'm running. There she is, our beautiful, innocent, pure baby girl. The reason I live. I see her smile and so I stop. I'm not even tired, I'm just happy. I don't want the moment to end. I'm staring at her and I just know that's how she's supposed to stay. Then suddenly a light appears ahead of me. It's so bright, Lewis. A huge great big spotlight. And inside the light, I see a face. This face seems familiar to me. And just as I'm trying to work out why my heart has gone warm at the sight of this man, the presence behind me gets stronger. Not only this, like a magnetic pull, my body is being dragged back. I'm trying hard, but I'm struggling to pull against the force and so I reluctantly turn around. Lewis, she's there."

"Who?"

"Jezebel." Closing her eyes, Eve shakes her head to remove the image from her mind. "I panic. I don't want her to have my daughter. I don't want her to taint my child, so I pull as hard as I possibly can and run towards the light. I'm desperately taking one step after another but the magnetic pull behind me is becoming stronger with every step I take. Jezebel's laughing. It's a cruel laugh that makes even Honey's little soul cry out. Then, from nowhere, I hear a voice bellow at me from the direction of the light. It's the man. He shouts, 'Darling, come here to me. I want to save you both!' And then just like that I wake up."

"Eve, that doesn't seem so bad. You just want to protect our daughter. I'm sure every mother feels the same way. I'm sure Sister Jesselle feels the same way about you as you do about Honey."

"Yes, but that's the thing – the man in the light. I'm certain he's my…"

"Your what…?"

"I'm certain he's my father. I'm certain he's Honey's grandfather."

CHAPTER 15

I Killed Them

"Brennan, keep up. We must be quick. We shouldn't be out here." Battling her way through the Moycullen Forest, Sister Alannah is in a hurry, "You really need to stay with me. We must be back no later than eight or the fact that we've left will be noticed and that isn't good."

True to her word that morning, Sister Alannah has taken Brennan out into the forest to try to find the lost recording device. With branches smacking her in the face, she's desperately trying to scramble her way through and ensure that Brennan remains behind her.

"Well, if you slow down, I might be able to keep up. Believe it or not, Sister Alannah, the last thing I want is to be stuck out here on my own again."

Frantic, as she doesn't want to be back late, Sister Alannah says, "Here, hold my hand."

Smiling, Brennan holds Sister Alannah's hand. "Can I ask you a question?"

Dragging Brennan as they venture deeper into the forest she says, "Yes – but only if you keep walking."

"You've just said that I was found way over there?"

"Yes."

"But that's nowhere near the gates."

"What do you mean?"

"Earlier today, you said that both yourself and Sister Kathryn found me outside the gates. Well, like I said, that's nowhere near the gates."

Unsure how to answer the question, Sister Alannah remains quiet. The pair continue to head deeper into the trees.

"Sister Alannah, answer the question, why are we heading this way if I was found outside the gates?" Brennan pulls his hand out of Sister Alannah's and stops, "I'm not moving another step until you answer my question."

"Brennan – you don't understand, I can't."

"What do you mean? You can't what? Sister Alannah, tell me what's going on." Walking over to her, Brennan places his hand on her cheek as he says, "Do you trust me?"

Closing her eyes and embracing the touch of his skin upon her face, Sister Alannah whispers, "Yes."

"I promise you can tell me anything."

Opening her eyes, Sister Alannah gazes deeply at Brennan, "Why did you come here?"

"What do you mean?"

"It's a very simple question – why did you come to the Moycullen Forest?"

"What has that got to do with what I've just asked you?"

"I just want to know."

"Okay, but you're the one that keeps saying we're in a rush and that we must hurry back, I'm a little confused as to what importance that particular question has to do with this moment right now. Do you want to enlighten me somewhat?"

"It's important and that's all you need to know."

Rolling his eyes and shaking his head, Brennan says, "Okay, if you think it's important, then fine, I'll answer you right now. It's simple, I just like to hunt the supernatural. I'm what people call a—"

"Paranormal hunter. I might live in a secluded nunnery but I'm not stupid, Brennan. You wanted to treat us like some sort of freak show?"

"I never implied that at all. Now you're just trying to put words in my mouth. Look, I'm just answering your question."

"Why don't I believe you?"

"Okay, fine, some dude I know called Tommy said that he grew up in this nunnery and he also said that I should come and see it in person because it's like nothing I'd ever experience. He told me that I might not make it out the forest alive but I really didn't care, I still don't, I just had to come and see this place for myself."

"And that's it?"

"Honestly, you're confusing me, Sister Alannah. Why is this such a big deal to you?"

"You'll see soon enough."

"What do you mean by that?"

"Right now you have no clue just how dark this universe is that you've just walked into. This place, this location you've chosen, chews individuals like you up and keeps them as its pets. Me asking you that particular question is me trying to find your motive for wanting to kill yourself, particularly when you say you're here to potentially find some ghosts." Sister Alannah lets out a sarcastic laugh as she continues, "To me, that just makes no logical sense. You're either dumb, immature or lying."

"Well, I guess I'm dumb or immature then, because it's the truth."

"So you expect me to believe that you flew all the way from New York in the hope that you might, what? Experience some paranormal activity and that's it?"

"Yeah."

"Brennan – why don't I believe you?"

"I don't know, but that's the reason."

"People try to find us all the time. People treat us like we're a freak show. Our holy nunnery gets taunted and looked at as though this is the home of Satan. All that poison, all that negative energy, all that hate has turned our once beautiful home into the real home for the unloved. I'm not even sure if our Lord can hear our prayers anymore. Each day we are forced to live in fear inside what feels like the house of horrors."

"Why can't you just leave?"

"I would never leave my sisters."

"Wait – how can people treat you like a freak show? Tommy said those who venture into the forest never return, he said those outside the forest believe that their loved ones have gotten lost and have died inside the forest somewhere. If what you're saying is true, then people have in fact found the nunnery?" After a brief moment of silence, Brennan continues, "If this is right, if they did find you, then why haven't you shown them their way home?" Still she says nothing. "Sister Alannah, why haven't you shown them how to get out of the forest?"

"Brennan, why do you hunt the supernatural?"

"If I answer your question, will you answer mine?"

"Yes."

"Do you promise?"

Holding his hands and looking deep into his eyes she says, "Brennan, you should be aware of one thing. If you lie to me, I will know; if you tell me the truth, I will know. I promise, if you answer my question honestly, I will warrant you the same respect back."

"Okay – this is going to be hard for me." Appearing slightly agitated, Brennan doesn't know if he should open up or not. "If I tell you my darkest secret, it's only because I trust you. And, well, you have no way of telling anyone I know."

"Brennan, please, tell me, let me help you."

"Okay – Sister Alannah, please do not judge me on what I am about to tell you."

"I won't, Brennan, I am a Sister to all, I am not here to judge. I am not allowed to judge. I am here to help and to heal. Please, trust me."

"The only way I can tell you this is if we create some sort of confession wall. I cannot look at you whilst I tell you this."

"That's fine, but I must remind you that we cannot be long. If you wish to find your electric device thingy, we are running low on time."

"I won't be long. You stand here and I'll stand over there."

There's now a tree between the two of them which is creating a barrier. Sister Alannah can no longer see Brennan.

"Sister Alannah, can you hear me?"

"Yes – Brennan, here there are no judgements. Here you can say what you need to free yourself. What is it that bothers you so much? And why is it that you seek clarity from the spirit world? What is it that makes you crave the hunting of the paranormal happenings amongst us where you place yourself in grave danger? Brennan, it's time, please talk to me."

Taking a deep breath in, Brennan knows he cannot continue to run from this dark secret forever. He knows it's only a matter of time before it kills him. This deep, dark secret is slowly eating away at his brain and is decaying every tiny individual thought he has. And not only this, this same dark secret has continually stopped him from sleeping for far too long now. Brennan knows it's time to share this burden he carries heavy on his shoulders.

With the thought process at the forefront of his mind, he breathes deep and bravely speaks, "So…" But unfortunately, his mind is unhelpfully stopping him from saying the words he wants to speak. Becoming more and more agitated, Brennan smacks himself in the head. "Arghhh, shut up, shut up, shut up. I'm doing this, I'm telling her."

"Brennan, are you okay?"

"Yes, I'm fine, it's just the voices in my head. You have to understand this has been a part of me and only me for such a long time now. Every inch of my being is telling me not to trust you. Not to tell you. But to be honest, I need to get it out. Whether you speak out or don't, I'm pretty sure I'm going to be dead anyway."

"Brennan, it's fine, you can tell me. I'm here for you."

Breathing deeply, Brennan finally plucks up the courage, breathes out and speaks once more, "I cannot believe I'm actually telling you this." With his head in his hands he continues, "So, it all started four years ago. I'd met the love of my life. She was my everything. You see, the older I got, the quicker my family dwindled away. I was the black sheep. The one that wasn't afraid to stand up for what was wrong about my upbringing. The one that dared to question the almighty adults. The one that wouldn't put up with anymore of the lies and the shit. Stood strong, they did. The ones who wronged me. Got me excluded from my family. Even my own parents couldn't give a fuck. They left me with no choice but to live without them. They were spreading poison, saying that I asked for everything I got. My so-called mother was the absolute worst. Stood by the side of her paedophile brother. And just like that, no more invites, no more birthday recognition, no more bullshit season's greetings and no more we wish you a happy New Year from anyone. Why? Because I decided to ask questions and get answers as to why I was in so many dangerous situations at such a young age and not one of them gave a flying fuck. I was called the tearaway teen who asked for it all. Ha, how does a twelve-year-old kid ask for a bad life? How does a kid ask to be given drink, drugs and be lured into sexual exploitation whilst under the influence? Answer me that one."

Sister Alannah remains silent.

"You see, you can't. Fear oozes from them all. They're scared because of what I know. I know my upbringing wasn't right. I didn't speak out then because I didn't know any better – but I'll be dammed if I won't speak out now. You see, it could have been so simple, they could have just recognised and apologised. Acknowledged – but instead they decided to blame me. How can people of that age not own their own shit? How can these people just get on with their daily life knowing how wrong they were and yet push it onto someone else? It's fucked up! And, instead of apologising and giving me answers, they ostracized me and continued to tell people that I asked for everything I got. Convinced them not to interact with me. Wonderful, that, isn't it? But oh no, these so-called extended family members won't raise their children the same way. Heaven forbid one of their kids walks the path they pushed me down. It's laughable, the word family. All because their mothers and fathers didn't give a fuck. So naturally, no-one gave a fuck about what was happening in our time." Laughing slightly, he says, "You wanna know how bad it actually gets?"

"Brennan, you don't have to…"

"No, it's fine, you've put me here now, I'm going to tell you. As I've mentioned, we have a paedophile uncle in the family. My mother's brother. He loved dating young teenage girls. I'm talking fresh out of elementary school. Thirteen-year-old maximum. Practically grooming them in front of everyone's eyes and this shit was acceptable. No one said a God damn thing. And yet, I speak out about it and I get cast aside like the reject. Well, they can shove their family up their fucking arses."

The anger, the hurt and the frustration are taking over. He's ready to lash out or cry. Desperate to regain control of his emotions, Brennan shakes his head, wipes his eyes and continues, "But that's by the by right now. That's not the reason I'm here. Well, it's part of the reason of how I got here, but not the entire reason. You see, one day I was just so beat up, so angry and so hurt, I'd honestly had enough of life. I went out to the nearest cliff. I had the biggest bottle of vodka in my hand. In my head, I had two very clear options, either to drink myself to death or throw myself off the cliff and to my immediate death. I chose to do both. I chose to drink the bottle and simply rock myself forward off the edge. And so I sat on the edge of the cliff, and I got more and more drunk with every sip. In fact, I was so drunk, at one point I was swaying slowly from side to side. I was ready to fall forward. And then suddenly I heard a voice. Then I felt a hand on my shoulder. Out of nowhere, I was pulled onto my back. Just a single second sooner and I would have gone over the edge. I opened my eyes, I was in a daze, but as clear as day, I saw her. Like an angel she had a glow behind her. Her mouth was moving but I couldn't hear the words she was speaking. I'd zoned out. All I could see was her beauty. I was saved by an angel. The most beautiful angel who would soon become the love of my life. I was saved by my Jannie."

A huge smile takes over his face as he relives this memory, "She was so beautiful and pure. She loved me for me. She loved me even though I didn't have a family. She loved me even though I was the only thing I brought to the table. I had nothing of value for her. I had a job that paid me well and a decent apartment in the city but that was it really. But Jannie didn't care about all that. She just wanted me. It felt amazing to be loved. To have someone share the same morals and values as I had. To know that I could live with her and not be judged. We'd been together for around two years and I confided in her. I told her what I'd been through. You see, I could see hurt behind her eyes. I could see that Jannie may have been through some form of trauma herself, but I didn't know what it was. I knew she had a dark secret like I did. Biting the bullet, I decided it was time. I was going to tell Jannie the truth. I knew she'd love me and not leave me. So I sat her down one evening and I told her. The look on her face told me everything I needed to know."

Putting his head down, Brennan swiftly wipes the tears away that have fallen down his face, "She didn't say a single word. She said nothing. She just reached out and gave me the biggest hug. For once in my life I felt loved and safe. I allowed myself to let go and I sunk into her arms. She held me for the longest time."

Brennan continues to wipe the tears that are now uncontrollably falling down his cheeks. He knows what's coming next, "That night she told me she was a victim of child abuse and continues to be a victim of adult abuse at the hands of her father. Not sexual abuse but physical abuse. He'd beaten her repeatedly. He would lock her away, throw things at her whilst she was in the cupboard and call her all sorts of abusive names. All her life she felt worthless. Her father's still living, you see. He'd always find a way to lure her home and then beat her. It was horrible. I'd say to her all the time, why do you go? But she just couldn't break free. It was programmed into her to fear this man and do as he said. But, little did we know, that was about to change. One day Jannie came to me and said that she had some news. I had no clue what it was but she seemed sad so I didn't think it was good news. For a moment I thought she was going to leave me. Jannie then told me she was pregnant. I remember falling back onto the chair and was gob smacked. I couldn't believe I was going to be a father. Me, damaged goods, I was going to have to take care of a child. The days passed and it slowly started to sink in. I was getting confident that I could be a good father regardless of my upbringing. I always knew Jannie would be an amazing mother. She knew she was going to be an amazing mother too, but something just wasn't sitting right with her. She was afraid. Jannie would cry most of the day and even sometimes sob in her sleep. She didn't know how she was going to protect our child when she couldn't even protect herself. Jannie didn't tell her father about the pregnancy at all. She couldn't, she said he would kill her. She stopped answering his calls and messages and from the minute she found out, she also stopped going around to his house. She knew if he beat her, the baby would never survive."

Brennan twiddles his fingers in silence for a moment then continues, "We had a scan and it told us we were having a boy. I started to get really excited. I was going to have a son. It all seemed so unreal. We decorated the nursery and got all his tiny clothes. And then…"

Wiping his face, Brennan's desperately trying not to choke on his tears. He's struggling to let the words come out of his mouth. Breathing out and being brave, he continues, "One day I woke up and she wasn't in the bed. I called her name and got no reply. She was gone. Not a trace of her in sight. I tried to call her friends, her work colleagues, I logged into her social media accounts, but nothing. It was as if she'd disappeared off the face of the earth. As a last resort I called her father. He answered the phone and I asked if he'd seen Jannie. He said one sentence that still sends chills down my spine. He said, "She's dead and so is that bastard son of yours." Brennan falls to the ground and cries in pain.

"Oh, Brennan, I'm so sorry." Sister Alannah says as she makes her way around the tree and kneels at the side of him.

Putting out her arms, she instantly begins cradling this broken man. The pair are silently kneeling in the dirt. The darkness of the night is beginning to fall. Surrounded by thick mud, Sister Alannah and Brennan are blending into the shadows of the Forest. They remain still, embracing each other. A moment or so passes. Regaining control of himself, Brennan wipes his face and pushes himself back from Alannah's hold.

Sister Alannah says, "Brennan… I… really… I just had no idea. I'm so sorry for digging and pushing you to share about such intimate and yet traumatising areas of your past. Honestly, I had no clue. I shall ask for forgiveness. I have indeed, misjudged you based on the others who have come here before you. I just thought you were like them. The ones who just come to make fun of us with their video cameras."

"You don't need to be sorry. After all, you didn't kill them, I practically did."

"No, no, no, no, no, you must never think like that. You did no such thing." Walking across to Brennan, Sister Alannah holds his head up by his chin, "You didn't do that to either of them. That horrible man took them away from you. You did nothing wrong."

"It just kills me. I feel no justice has been served for them. No reason for taking them away from me."

"Did you phone the Police?"

"Yes, her father's currently in prison awaiting trial. The horrible bastard pleaded not guilty so I have to stay alive and attend the trial to get justice for them both. He won't even say where he's put their bodies. I'm grateful that the cops were able to lock him up based on evidence they found during the investigation. There were multiple messages sent and calls made. They also found fresh blood splatter in his house – Jannie's blood. They determined it matched with the timeline of her disappearance. Every day I pray that I can make contact with them both in the spiritual world. Every day I pray that Jannie can give me the answers he's refusing to give. Every day I pray that maybe, just maybe, I'll find their bodies and lay them both to rest. After all, it's the least I can do, I basically killed them."

"Brennan, how can you believe that? You did not kill them, that monster did."

"He might have taken her last breath, but I didn't protect her or my son. She knew her dad would kill her, she pretty much warned me that he would do it and I didn't take her seriously."

"But really, what could you have done? He would have found her one day regardless."

"I could have moved us out the state, I could have saved her. I could have saved my son, I could have done something and yet I sat back and I let it happen. History repeating. I'm still just the same kid I was years ago. I let those vile mother fuckers take my innocence and I let this vile bully take the love of my life and our son. Do you know how hard it is to live with this? All I want to do is go back to that cliff and this time fall forward."

CHAPTER 16

The Clock is Ticking

The grounds of the nunnery are quiet. Not a sound can be heard. The trees are still. Brennan and Sister Alannah have made it back to the nunnery undetected. The clock has struck ten p.m. and it's almost time for all the nocturnal animals to make an appearance. Up high, the sky is a blanket of black. Not a single star can be seen. The moon is beaming at full capacity, showing off in all its glory. It's so big, so beautiful and so near it almost feels close enough to touch. The chapel front is gloomy and uninviting. Everything is overgrown and thick. The ivy on the exterior walls has taken over the brick and has begun travelling down the pathway and the steps. The fast-spreading vegetation is so long it could easily wrap itself around your body twice. The huge, dark brown wooden doors are closed. A thick silver chain and padlock sits tightly around the steel handles, securely binding the two doors together. As the wind blows, the chain and padlock begin to rattle. It almost sounds as if someone is knocking at the door. Sister Jennifer stands by the front steps of the chapel holding a lantern in one hand and cradling sleeping baby Honey who has just been baptised in the other. At her side, also holding a lantern and cradling baby Hope, is Sister Cathleen. The two sisters look at each other and smile.

"Young love, Sister. Oh, what I would have done with such a thing," Sister Jennifer says, her voice low.

118

"Huh, what did you say, Sister?"

"I was saying about young love. Sister Cathleen, what do you think it feels like to have someone in this world love you like that? Do you ever think about how life could have been?"

"Yes – I do sometimes. I think about what it might feel like to have someone hold my face and tell me they love me."

"Sister, do you ever think we should have lived our lives differently?"

"Whatever do you mean?"

"I'm just saying, you know, if we hadn't been so hasty in giving all of our eternity to our Father. If we had left the home when we hit adulthood and lived a while instead of making the decision to stay in the confinement of the nunnery, who knows, we could have gone exploring. Seen the world the way others do, maybe found love, maybe become different women…"

"Yes, Sister, I often wonder, but then I instantly ask for forgiveness as I have promised my life to our Father, and who am I to even consider breaking that promise. When I have those moments of weakness or uncertainty, I have to remind myself that he is my one true love."

"I guess you're right, Sister," Sister Jennifer says with a heavy sigh. The pair stand in silence. Both appear to be deep in thought. Their whole lives, all they have known is the Moycullen Nunnery. The only ground they have walked upon is in this one small place upon the huge planet. The Moycullen Forest are the grounds most of these women and men were born on. Of course, most of the residents here have heard tales of the rest of the world but a large percentage of them have never ventured too far from home. These residents can only dream about the stories which sound so beautiful and spiritually enhancing. The stories that give them a burning desire to run off and go see the world with their own eyes. Be free, take that plunge of faith. Run through the forest and never look back. Smiles growing on their faces. Hearts beating as they chase a new existence. Adrenaline surging throughout their bodies. Laughing as they throw their habits and veils on the ground. Glowing in their own happiness as they finally reach the end of the forest. And there they stand. But, like every fairy tale story, waiting in the midst of happiness and desperate to pounce, is the darkness that lives amongst the world, ugly and uninviting. Nuns, workers, residents and visitors over the years have come and left stories of the outside world. Some of the tales speak about the merciless evil that exists throughout the world. These tales hold no hope for a better life. These stories tell a cruel, cold version of the world. This is what holds them back. Shuddering at the thought, Sister Jennifer doesn't believe the risk is worth taking.

Standing centre place at the front of the chapel and pacing up and down is Sister Marie, "Has anybody seen Sister Alannah? She should have been here for Honey's baptism," she says.

"No. Would you like me to go look for her?" Sister Jennifer asks.

"No, Sister. Sister Briana has gone to find her. But for now, we will have to continue without her. We mustn't be outside much longer or our absence will be noticed."

Sister Marie sees a small flickering light appearing from out of the distance. Gradually, the tiny ball of light gets brighter as it travels towards them. The rustling of leaves and grass and snapping twigs can also be heard. The angelic light is now in close proximity, and Sister Marie decides to go and investigate.

"What shall we do, Sister Marie? What is that?" Sister Jennifer asks.

"Just stay calm, Sister Jennifer. It could be Sister Alannah and Sister Briana. Everyone just stay put, I'm going to see what it is."

Looking to Lewis, Eve says, "You don't think it's…"

"No."

"It better not be, Lewis, or we're dead."

Sister Marie sets off towards the light. As she gets closer, she can hear a prominent huffing and puffing. She stands still and squints. Seeing an oversized, female figure rushing towards her with rounded glasses perched upon her nose, Sister Marie eventually works out that it is Sister Briana. She looks tired and her puffy face is red. She puts one of her hands on her knee, trying to catch her breath.

"My goodness, Sister, you gave us all a fright," Sister Marie says. "Did you find her? We've had to baptise the baby without her presence, we had no choice."

"Sorry, Sister, I came to say that I cannot find Sister Alannah." Still trying to catch her breath, Sister Briana is now bent over with both of her hands on her knees. She looks up at Sister Marie, breathing deeply. "Sister Faith was on her way to check the children and she said that... that... she last saw her sneaking around with the boy from America."

Rolling her eyes in disapproval, Sister Marie turns and begins marching back towards the others, "Not to worry. We are going to have to perform the wedding ceremony without her too. Follow me." she tells Sister Briana.

"Yes, that's all good and well, but... hang on..."

"What? Will you just catch your breath and follow me, Sister."

"Just wait. You should know that I think Sister Elisabeth saw me... leaving."

"How? Sister, you didn't let her follow, did you?"

"No, of course not." Pulling herself up, Sister Briana continues, "She was watching from her window. I caught her staring at me. I carried on walking and then when I glanced back, she'd gone. I've been checking the whole way over here and no one has been following me, I'm certain."

"We must hurry!"

Sister Marie hurries back to the group. She knows that time is no longer on their side. They need to return to the nunnery as soon as possible. Sister Marie doesn't wish to ruin the moment and so she shares a great big smile. She knows her mission outweighs her fear. Her strong faith encourages her and tells her that it is imperative that the task in hand is to be completed.

Eve and Lewis are feeling no anxiety whatsoever. They are embracing the moment, standing hand in hand, wearing smiles that radiate from ear to ear. The bride and groom are ready to make their promise to one another by reciting their vows of marriage. The pair look almost angelic against the glow from the lanterns. You would never believe evil runs through any of their veins. Love, purity and innocence captivated in one moment. A moment when time stands still for the pair of them. A moment in this lifetime where everything and everyone seems irrelevant. A moment for the two of them to connect as one. Tears begin to fall down Eve's face. Tears of joy and pure happiness. She's only dreamed that she could feel this kind of connection, the connection that humans feel when they fall in love. Eve *never* thought it would happen to her. And yet here she stands, hand in hand, beaming from the love that flows through her heart.

"I, Lewis Parkinson, take thee, Evelyn Jade Honey, to be my wedded wife, to have and to hold, from this day forward, for better, for worse, for richer, for poorer, in sickness and in health, to love and to cherish, till death do us part."

"Lewis if you could now place the chosen ring onto Eve's finger," Sister Marie says with a smile on her face.

Confused as they don't have rings, Eve peers at Sister Briana as she steps forward. She's holding a tiny silk cushion, on which, placed beautifully and tied loosely by silk ribbon, are two dark oak wedding bands.

"I told Mark about your upcoming nuptials. I thought it would be best if we had a set of eyes over the nunnery whilst we are out. Don't worry, he's vowed to keep it secret. He did not want you to get wedded without a band. He whittled these out of oak some time ago and he wanted you both to have them. A wedding gift from him."

Eve is speechless, her hand over her mouth.

"Now, Lewis, if you can take the ring for me and place it on Eve's finger."

Sister Briana holds out with the white silk cushion to Lewis. Tears begin to trickle slowly down Sister Briana's face. Taking the ring from the cushion, Lewis beams as he glides the ring onto Eve's finger.

Eve sobs as she recites her vows. She cannot believe she has married her best friend. Placing the ring onto Lewis's finger, Eve is eager to kiss her husband.

"I now pronounce you man and wife. Lewis, you may kiss your bride."

Lewis kisses his wife, wrapping his arms around Eve's neck and holding her tightly. "It's always been you, baby," he whispers in her ear.

Placing the tip of her nose onto his, Eve lets out the biggest sigh of relief. Now they are finally whole. Now they can be a family.

"Sister Jennifer, please can you pass me my baby?" Sister Eve says.

"Of course, Sister."

"Please, call me Mrs. Parkinson."

Smiling, Sister Jennifer says, "Of course, Mrs. Parkinson." Making her way across to the newlyweds, Sister Jennifer passes baby Honey to her mother. "Here is your daughter."

Cradling her baby girl and holding her new husband, Eve has never been this happy. She kisses her daughter on her tiny warm head and Lewis joins her. Tears fall from their faces and land onto Honey's. Giggling, they look at their wedding bands and kiss each other whilst crying. The moment is perfect.

CHAPTER 17

Too Close to Home

The weeks have passed quickly. It's the morning of twenty-eighth of June. Matthew is getting anxious as the seventh of July is fast approaching. After no known sightings of Eve or any of Phil's missing children, Matthew and Phil have had various meetings in secret with DCS Terry at Matthew's home. Each of them is unsure of what direction to take. At their last meeting, which took place just a few days ago, it was decided that they should take a trip to visit one of DCS Terry's previous colleagues who worked closely with him on the initial investigation of Matthew Honey – Operation Bee Sting. DCS Terry stands in the reception area at the Lockstock Psychiatric Hospital.

"Hi, we're here to see Maria Flores," he says to the receptionist.

"Sure, sign in here, please," she replies. "How many people have you brought with you?"

"Two others." DCS Terry turns and says, "Matthew, Phil, you gotta sign your names 'ere, lads."

Matthew doesn't hear DCS Terry. He's in a daze, bewildered by his surroundings. Feeling a tap on his shoulder, Matthew turns.

"Matthew, you need to sign your name 'ere," DCS Terry repeats.

Matthew remains silent as he signs himself in. He stares at the walls. There are posters of all different sizes plastered everywhere. One of them reads: *Don't Believe Everything Your Brain Tells You!*

Another, just behind the reception area, reads: *Have you taken your medication today?*

Glancing over his shoulder, Matthew notices there's a sea of patients walking freely around the reception area. They all share the same appearance. With their pale complexions, the majority look as if they haven't seen the sun for months. They wear dreary clothes and their hair is overgrown. Matthew cannot stop himself from staring. Some of them are talking and mumbling to themselves underneath their breath. Matthew begins to sweat. This place is bringing back some very bad memories for him and he doesn't like it one bit.

Shaking his head to try and regain his composure, Matthew whispers in Phil's ear, "Phil, I don't know if I can do this."

"Sorry, what did you say?"

"I said, I don't think I can be 'ere. I need to leave."

"You'll be fine, mate. Honestly, don't worry."

"Phil, seriously, it's kicking up some internal shit for me. I ain't meant to be 'ere."

"Just try and stay calm. Don't freak out. Honestly, I've got your back. Just go sit over there. I'm sure it won't be long."

"You're havin' a laugh if you think I'm walking anywhere near over there. Not being funny, mate, but 'ave you had a look around? It's like the walking dead in 'ere."

"Sshh, Matthew, lower your voice. You can't say that, it's proper disrespectful."

"I really don't give a fuck. It's making me uncomfortable."

"Come on, mate, just keep it together, we won't be long. And, you never know, we might get something useful out of this meeting. Just keep it together for a little bit longer."

"I don't know if I can, Phil. It's playing with my head."

"Mate, come on, we've been through way worse than this. We both nearly ended up in one of these hospitals, we should just be grateful that we were able to get better without having to be admitted here. Now come on mate, stop being stupid and pull yourself together. You've got this. Just remember why we're here."

Realising that Phil's right, Matthew closes his eyes and tries to regain control over his thoughts. Slowly breathing deeper and deeper,

Matthew desperately tries not to freak out. With his back turned away from Phil and DCS Terry, Matthew takes his final deep breath, counts back from five and then slowly opens his eyes. Matthew notices a male patient in the centre of the seating area. He's acting strangely as compared to the rest of the patients. His behaviour is suspicious. He's stroking the walls. And keeps looking over his shoulder. He is wearing brown cord trousers, a brown stripy cardigan and has dark brown greasy hair that rests upon his shoulders. He's at least six feet tall and appears to be in his mid-twenties, with an innocent looking, youthful complexion. It's hard for Matthew to comprehend how such a young man has ended up in this place. Watching his every movement, Matthew sees the young male slowly dragging his heavy body around the reception area. He shuffles along, making very slow progress. Watching attentively, Matthew senses this particular patient is on some type of mission. The young male is heading for the exit. Panicking, Matthew's unsure of what he should do. Surely this man can't escape? Matthew taps Phil on the shoulder.

Phil doesn't turn, he's too busy speaking with DCS Terry and the lady at reception, "One second, mate, they're having trouble finding my details," he says to Matthew. "Be with you in a sec, just keep breathing deep. You'll be fine."

Matthew puts his hand on his head. He's not sure what to do next. Should he grab a staff member to tell them or just start shouting to alert them? Watching the young male pick up his pace, Matthew sees he's not far from the exit. Taking a deep breath in, Matthew decides to do nothing. He's somewhat intrigued. He's pondering the possibility of escaping such a place… is it really this easy? The male patient is now only a few more steps away from freedom. Slowly, the male turns around, appearing to make sure he is not being followed. Seemingly assured, he scans the area one last time and makes eye contact with the only person watching him – Matthew. He smiles at him. Smiling back, Matthew slowly puts his hand up and gives the young male a tiny wave goodbye. Just two metres from the exit, this young male appears to be excited. He reaches out and grabs the metal door handle. As soon as he pulls it down, the door *clicks*. The doors are then immediately bolted, triggering the alarm system, which begins blasting throughout the ward. The rest of the patients become distressed by the horrific ear-piercing sound. Some of the nurses attempt to soothe the residents. Five nurses – two female, and three male, all dressed in pale green uniforms – rush over and restrain the wannabe escapee, tackling him to the ground. It's almost painful to watch. Matthew has gone from feeling anxious about this facility to having empathy for those around him. Yes, this has brought up some very close, very disturbing memories, but, this isn't his story. Like Phil said, he wasn't confined like these people are. He was one of the lucky ones who pulled through. Matthew sees the nurses push the young man's head to the ground and hold him tightly. He once again makes eye contact with Matthew. This time he looks so sad and deflated. He's saying nothing, just staring at Matthew. A tear rolls down Matthew's cheek.

Suddenly, Phil taps Matthew on the shoulder, "Mate, you alright?"

Matthew responds to Phil with a slight nod of the head. He's far from alright but he's not about to tell anyone.

"Okay, well we're about to go down now, they found my details so we can all go through. You ready, mate?"

"Erm, yeah. I'm coming now."

Matthew smiles one last time at the young male. This time it's a smile of compassion. Once again feeling a tap on his shoulder, Matthew turns.

"Mate, come on. We're ready."

"Yeah, sure, I'm right behind ya."

A nurse steps out from behind the counter. She has short, choppy blonde hair with a fringe that rests just above her eyebrows. Her eyes are bright blue and she looks like she has just come back from a vacation as she has a very tanned complexion. In one hand she has a clipboard and in the other she has visitor badges.

"Hi, I'm Nurse Kimble. Please put these on. If you're not wearing one, I should warn you, you may find yourself slung in one of our residential rooms." Laughing, Nurse Kimble passes each of them a visitor's necklace, "Oh and be very careful if you're using the bathroom. Some of our longstanding patients have been known to prey on guests for these visitor badges. They think they're going to be able to trick us into letting them out."

Looking to Phil and Matthew, DCS Terry says, "So, no using the bathroom then."

"Now, before I take you down, I must also advise you, there are cameras present everywhere. You are being recorded at all times. The forms you signed earlier have permitted us to record you during your time in our facility. As I'm sure each of you can appreciate, this is a high security establishment and so we must ensure that we have eyes and ears everywhere at all times for everyone's safety. The only places we do not record are the toilet cubicles along with the bath and shower areas. There are two-way mirrors present in a vast majority of the rooms. As I said, you will be watched at all times."

"You guys ain't messing around."

"DCS Terry, safety is of paramount importance here. Not only for our residents, but staff and visitors too. You have no idea how dangerous and strong some of these individuals are."

"Believe me, I can imagine."

"Okay, if you'd like to follow me, gents."

They follow Nurse Kimble in silence. Looking to Phil, Matthew notices he appears to be just as bewildered as he is. Matthew takes in his surroundings. The ceilings and walls are extremely high. Resting at the top are small rectangular windows. They let in a small amount of natural sunlight, which bounces off the walls. The walls have been painted a calming light shade of blue. Fluffy clouds adorn the ceiling and the tops of the walls, while the bottom of the walls are decorated with authentic-looking grass and flowers. There are birds dotted throughout the mural, as though they are flying high, and silhouettes of people on the grass holding hands. It looks like a truly peaceful summer's day. Although, Matthew cannot help but notice the smell circulating is far from that of a fresh summer's day. It's a strong stench of sterile chemicals. As they continue down the extremely long corridor, they begin to hear the moans, pleas and cries from the residents locked behind their doors.

"Oh, don't mind them. These are some of our residents that have been locked in segregation for their own safety."

Curious, Matthew asks, "Is that what will happen to the young male who was just trying to escape?"

"Who? Denny?"

"Is that his name?"

"Yeah – oh Denny, we all love him. He's been with us for the past four years now."

"What four years, really? He only looks about mid-twenties, he's so young."

"He is. Denny's one of our younger residents. He's always trying to escape. It's sad because it's a vicious cycle for him. We segregate him, he gets out and then he does it again."

"Is there no way he can leave? I mean, what does it take to get out of a place like this?"

"Well, ultimately, that's not our decision. We just look after the patients. They each have their own assigned consultant who assesses them on a regular basis. We don't really get told the end date. We just look after them until they leave to go home or to another less secure facility. I'm certain that as soon as Denny makes the right progress, they'll look to do the same thing with him."

"Oh."

"Erm, Nurse Kimble?" DCS Terry chips in.

"Please call me Penny."

"Thanks. Penny, how's Maria doing?"

"Well, it actually saddens me to say this, but Maria has had a rough few days. Her moods are very unpredictable, and if truth be told, we were debating about whether to let you come to see her at all."

"What do you mean a rough few days?"

"Just a real hard time for her recently. She's not settling at night-time at all. She keeps crying out and ripping at her eyelids. I'm told it's the same time every night. As soon as the darkness falls and it hits her room. From what I've been advised, it appears to have become a very distinctive pattern."

This statement has instantly grasped Matthew's attention, "What do you mean always at night-time? What does she say is happening?"

"Erm, I mean I'm not one hundred percent certain, I'd have to check her notes as I'm her daytime supervisor. But during handover, my colleagues have reported that she's always highly distressed during the night. It's like a whole change in personality. She struggles, screams, bangs on the door and the window to be let out. She refuses to sleep. She's not much better in the day, either, although there is a slight improvement. It's like she's scared to close her eyes. Honestly, this poor, poor, woman, she's so tired. You can see she's exhausted. And as we know, what comes with exhaustion? A tendency to suffer with delusional experiences. It's just such a shame. A beautiful young woman with a bright future ahead of her. I always find our PTSD cases are the saddest."

"Yeah, believe me, during my time in the Force I've seen many go this way."

"It's very sad."

Looking to Phil, Matthew is certain this can only mean one thing – Maria is being visited in the night. Matthew's nervous but ready to find out what she knows and what she has seen.

"Mate, do you think it's you know who?" Matthew says to Phil.

"Put it this way – if it ain't, then I'm the Pope," Phil replies.

As they continue down the corridor they're soon greeted by a royal blue sign that has two white arrows. One pointing to the left and one pointing to the right.

Looking at her clipboard Nurse Kimble says, "Okay, so I believe Maria will have been transported to the Cambridge Suite by now. So, if you'd like to follow me."

She reaches out her hand, placing her chipped wristband in front of the door. Matthew hears the clicking of the mechanisms inside as they unlock the door. Guiding them through, Nurse Kimble looks to the camera and says, "They're with me."

As they walk through the doorway, Nurse Kimble then closes the door behind her. She lifts the handle and her wristband initiates the lock.

"Please, follow me."

Leading the way, Nurse Kimble smiles at some colleagues as they pass by.

Matthew feels like he has been walking for miles. He had no clue that the hospital was so big. Once they reach the end of the corridor, they approach another secured section. Opening the doorway to the reception area, Nurse Kimble again looks to the camera and says, "They're with me."

"You have to say that every single time?" Phil asks.

"Yeah, we can have staff changes, different cameras being watched by different people. It's hard for them to keep track of one journey so it's mandatory that we confirm our safety when it comes to visitors with each camera."

"Wow, I never knew it had to be so tight," Phil replies.

"We are looking at some very sick people. As I've said, your safety and theirs is of paramount importance."

With a shocked expression upon his face, Phil continues, "I mean, I know, I'm like really grateful, but I just never imagined it would actually be, you know, this secure. Especially having only seen places like this in movies."

Giggling, Nurse Kimble shakes her head and smiles as she makes her way across to the reception desk.

Standing still, DCS Terry, Matthew and Phil begin taking in their new surroundings. Matthew notices that the layout is remarkably like the reception area they have just left. Although, this time, there is one distinctive difference… there are no patients walking freely. This area is secluded and has only staff members present.

Standing at the front desk and waiting for the receptionist, Nurse Kimble shouts, "Miriam, where's Thea?"

Making her way to the desk, Nurse Miriam replies, "I'm not sure, I think she might have just gone to the bathroom. What's it I can help you with?"

"We've got three visitors to see Maria Flores, in the Byrne lounge on the Cambridge Suite, so I believe. Is this still the case?"

"Let me check." Tapping away on her computer, Nurse Miriam says, "Just bear with me one second." Picking up the telephone, Nurse Miriam speaks to someone the other end.

Matthew is getting antsy. He can hear the moans, groans and screams of the residents echoing throughout. It's an almost eerie sound. He shudders.

"What the fuck have you brought us to?" Matthew says to DCS Terry.

"Matthew, just calm down. I need all eyes on this."

"Calm down? I feel like I'm in a fuckin' nightmare."

"Not being funny, Terry, but I don't feel much safer about this," Phil says nervously.

"Right, stop being a pair of fuckin' pussies and focus. We're here to get information about what she saw and why she's in 'ere. Now suck it up cause it ain't my kids that demonic bitch has taken so I can just go home if I want. I ain't arsed. Now are you gonna stop being a pair of wet vaginas and crack on or are you gonna bail? Your call. I couldn't give a fuck anymore. I've 'ad enough of babysitting you two muppets."

Matthew feels bad for his behaviour. He realises he has lost sight of the real reason they are there, "No, you're right, I'm sorry. It's really kicking a lot of shit up for me this. Too close to home, that's all. I'll pull myself together, don't worry."

"Yeah, me too," says Phil. "Sorry, Terry."

Getting off the call, Nurse Miriam says, "Okay, so Maria took a turn for the worse in the night. She's no longer able to sit in one of our lounges. She has been spoken to and she would like to speak with your visitors, but for their safety and hers this is now going to take place behind the protective enclosed visits section. If you could just make your way towards the Starlight Ward by following the gold feet."

"Thank you very much, Miriam," Nurse Kimble says. Waving her clipboard, she says, "Come on, follow me." As they catch up to her, Nurse Kimble continues, "Okay, so you heard what Miriam said. You're no longer in one of the lounges for your safety and Maria's — instead, you're going to be visiting via our secure section which has secure window panes throughout."

"What do you mean for our safety and hers?"

"Well, as you heard Miriam say, Maria took a turn for the worst last night. The visit would ordinarily be cancelled, but I guess she's hell bent on seeing you three, so I'm assuming that's why you're being permitted to go ahead with your visit."

"Penny, I just can't believe it, I'm still in shock at times," DCS Terry says. "She's such a bonny young girl you know, it's hard to believe this is where she has ended up."

"I know. All we can ask is that you please be patient. And please bear in mind when you see her that she's not her normal self. You must take into consideration the fact that she is sick and needs support and shouldn't be grilled right now. That might help her go a long way with recovery."

"Sure, that's not a problem. We will be very mindful about what we say during our chat."

"Just don't put any undue pressure on her, please."

"I worked with her side by side for a long period of time. I consider her a friend, not just a colleague. You have my word, I will not put any undue pressure on her. Nor will the other two."

"Thank you. Okay, if you'd please follow me, gents. I'll show you to the room."

Nurse Kimble leads DCS Terry, Matthew and Phil into a room that is empty, apart from three uncomfortable looking chairs placed in front of a huge window. The thick, bulletproof glass goes from the ceiling right down to the floor. The room on the other side of the glass has one of the same uncomfortable looking chairs in it. The décor on both sides matches the summer's day theme of the corridors. Up high, there are multiple black speakers built into the walls and spread out around the rooms. Also up high are multiple microphones. This internal system has been built to enable the patients and their visitors to communicate effectively whilst ensuring everyone's safety. There are no pictures on the wall or items in the room other than the chairs.

As they take their seats, Nurse Kimble says, "Maria will be with you in a just minute." She then leaves the room.

DCS Terry sits in anticipation, breathing deeply. Will she make it to the visit, or won't she? The tension is building as he looks to the watch on his wrist and sees the time passing by. Not a word is spoken between the three of them. Around ten minutes later, the door handle on the other side of the glass is pulled down. Slowly, the door begins to open. The speaker suddenly crackles to life and they hear a voice say, "It's this way, Maria. Just take your time now, we don't want you to trip."

This is followed by a female voice shouting, "Oh, fuck off, Derek, you patronizing prick. Let me in now."

DCS Terry smiles. He knows exactly who that voice belongs to – DC Flores. Hearing her stand up for herself makes him happy. A man, who must be Derek, enters the room. He doesn't appear to be as happy.

"Now that isn't very nice, is it Maria?"

"Derek, you really wanna stay out my face today. Now let me in the room."

"Okay – well I'm just—"

"Oh, fuck off, Derek. Just let me in the room, you jobs-worth muppet."

Derek rolls his eyes.

Taking another deep breath, DCS Terry sits up straight. Matthew and Phil mirror his actions. With their backs straight in their seats they all look like rabbits in headlights. DCS Terry is getting more and more anxious about DC Flores's entrance. Suddenly, he sees her walk into the room. Almost instantly, DCS Terry begins smiling. Although she might not look exactly how he remembered her, nonetheless, he can still see as clear as daylight, that's his girl right there. That's his feisty DC Flores. She's wearing a pair of off-white, thick, grubby looking trousers, complemented by an off-white, ghastly, weighted restraint jacket. The clothing is oversized and buries her tiny frame. Her thick, chocolate-brown hair is long and doesn't look like it's seen a brush for months, let alone shampoo.

As she enters the room, Maria immediately spots DCS Terry and smiles. Rushing to the glass, she shouts, "Terry – you came. You really came. It's really you. It's really you. I knew you'd come to save me from these arseholes." She stares at Derek, "You can fuck off now, Derek."

"I can't, Maria, you know that," Derek responds, rolling his eyes. "Nurse Goma advised that I must oversee your visit, otherwise it would not be permitted. We literally just had a conversation about it before I opened the door and you agreed."

"Yeah, well, don't think you can chip in. You just stand in the corner like a good boy while I talk to my friends."

Standing at the glass, Maria puts her head on it and says, "I've missed you."

"I've missed you too."

"Oh, how I've missed hearing your cockney voice," she responds, smiling.

DCS Terry smiles back at her with a cheeky grin.

Maria glances to the side of DCS Terry, "Oh my goodness, Matthew, Phil, hello! Thank you for coming."

Matthew and Phil exchange a confused look. She's making it sound like she has invited them all for tea. They smile back at her.

"How are you all doing?" Maria asks.

"Maria, why don't you take a seat and then we can talk," DCS Terry says, taking charge of the conversation.

"Yeah, yeah, of course."

Maria walks backwards very slowly, without taking her eyes off them. Smiling, she takes a seat. Getting a proper look at her, DCS Terry is extremely concerned. Her tanned complexion is no more, her skin is pale. She has scratches that extend from her eyelids down to her cheeks. Some appear old and some look new, with fresh blood at the top of the wounds. The rings around her eyes are dark. They almost look like black eyes. Her face is very gaunt and she looks like she hasn't eaten for weeks. Hanging heavy at either side of her face, her hair appears matted and is overgrown. DCS Terry is sickened by this image. This once radiant-looking woman is now the complete opposite. She looks very sick. Saddened, but trying to remain professional, DCS Terry closes his eyes and thinks to himself, *Come on, Terry, it's not your fault she's in here. Just pull yourself together, lad*. Breathing deep, he decides to lead the conversation by engaging in some friendly chit chat, "So, how they treatin' ya? I'm guessing from Derek at the back there you ain't so happy."

"Nah, he's alright. They're just chimps doing what they're told. You must at least try to negotiate or what's the point, right? You taught me that, Terry."

Smiling, he says, "Sure did."

"Erm Maria," Matthew butts in. "Penny, erm, Nurse Kimble said that you've been having a rough time at night. Is that true?"

Furious, DCS Terry gives Matthew a what-the-fuck-did-you-ask-that-for look. He wanted to sweet talk her into getting some answers, not jump right in and scare her off, "Maria, you don't need to answer that," he says.

"No, Terry, it's alright," Maria says. "I want to help as much as I can. We're all part of this investigation. We can solve it together, right?"

Feeling proud, DCS Terry smiles at her strength. "That's right. We can."

"Yes, Nurse Kimble's right, I have been having a rough time at night. You see, I'm not crazy, I promise. I just can't cope with her. She constantly visits me."

Matthew gets up from his seat and asks tersely, "Who visits you? Jezebel? Is it her?"

"You need to get a grip of yourself, lad," DCS Terry says, pushing Matthew back into his seat. "Calm down or go sit out in the corridor. You're not helping."

"I'm just trying to—"

"Listen, we all want the same result, so just compose yourself and ask questions calmly or leave it to me."

"Okay, I'm sorry." Looking to Maria, Matthew says, "I just really want to get my daughter back. I haven't seen her for twenty-three months. I'm getting more desperate with every day that goes by that I haven't found her. I apologise, Maria, I shouldn't be so blunt."

"Don't worry, Terry, I want to help. Let me help, please. Matthew, it's okay, I understand. Just because I'm in here please don't think I'm not normal because I am. They just don't want to believe me, like they didn't believe you."

Matthew raises his eyebrows as he whispers, "Ain't that the truth."

"Anyway, no, it isn't Jezebel. It's Alice."

Phil instantly sits up at the sound of his wife's name. "Sorry, what did you just say? My wife visits you in the night?"

"Yeah, Phil. Your wife visits me every night," Maria says.

"Wait… why? What for? I don't understand," Phil splutters.

Maria swings her feet, looking at the floor. She seems to have drifted off into a daze.

"Maria?" DCS Terry says gently. "Are you okay?"

"Erm, yeah."

"Do you think you can tell us what's happening at night between you and Alice?"

Maria takes a deep breath then starts to talk, "The night we found Alice's body, you were stood outside discussing something with someone and I decided to go back inside the house to check one final time for anything that could potentially explain what had happened or even just a tiny shred of evidence. As I walked through the doorway, I thought I heard a woman's voice coming from the dining room where Alice was. I don't know why but I thought it might have been Alice. For a brief moment I thought we might have got it wrong. In that one tiny moment of hope, I thought that Alice was still alive. I didn't even think, I just ran into the room. As I entered the room, I saw Alice's body still lay on the floor. I walked up to her and it was very clear to me that she wasn't alive. Her fingers had gone blue and the blood that had dripped down them was now starting to crust. Confused, because I'd definitely heard a woman's voice groaning, I decided to check her pulse on her wrist just to be sure there wasn't a slight beat. As I touched her skin, it was like a surge of electricity travelled throughout my body. I was flung across the room and I banged my head. I'm not sure how long I was out cold for, but when I came round, Alice was leaning over me." Maria sits forward and bounces her leg up and down, then begins rocking back and forth slowly.

"Maria, it's okay, we're here. You don't need to be afraid," DCS Terry reassures her. "I'm sorry that you had to see that, but it's okay now, you're safe. Just try to stay calm. Breathe deeply, everything's going to be okay. Okay?"

Looking at DCS Terry, Maria continues, "Terry, her face was horrific. Honestly, it was so scary. I gasped and I tried to shout but I was petrified. I could see the blood that had drained from her neck. She had deep red blood stains down her chest. Her eyes were soulless and yet there she stood, just staring at me."

"Maria, it's okay. You're doing great. You're really helping us to solve this case. I'm extremely proud of you."

"Maria, what happened then? Did she say anything to you?" Phil asks.

"She tried but she couldn't get the words out. She couldn't speak."

"Wait, I'm confused," Matthew intervenes. "So why do you think she's visiting you if she can't speak?"

"I don't know, maybe to taunt me because I lived and she didn't? Maybe I've been cursed from the electric shock I got from her corpse. Who knows why she's choses to visit me. All I do know is that I can't sleep and life is getting very exhausting very quickly for me."

"I'm sorry," Matthew says.

"Every time I close my eyes and drift off to sleep, I see that sickening room. I smell the stench of rotting flesh and dried blood. I can't get it out my mind, no matter how hard I try to fight it. It's like it's stained on my brain."

"Maria, what happens when my wife visits you?" Phil asks.

"It's the same dream every time. The same scenario. It's like my brain has lost all capacity to dream of anything else."

"Have you ever stayed asleep long enough to try and work out what she might want or what she might be trying to share with you?" Matthew asks.

"No – I haven't. I freak out and instantly wake myself up. I scream, I shout and I just want to get out my room in case she appears and there's no one around to help me. I just don't want to be alone."

Looking to DCS Terry and Matthew, Phil lowers his voice and says, "I think Alice is trying to tell Maria something. We have to try and convince her to sleep."

"Mate, I think you're right," Matthew agrees. "Terry, we need to get her to sleep. We need to get her to speak with Alice or follow her. I think Phil's right, she's trying to tell her something or show her something. She trusts you, you need to try to convince her to stay asleep. This might be the only lead we can get."

Trying to process what Matthew has just said, DCS Terry takes a deep breath in. He ponders how on earth he should approach this. He can see Maria is clearly highly traumatised by what she has already witnessed and he's worried what the cost will be for this sacrifice. Looking through the glass, he can see just talking about this has already had a severe impact on her mental state. She's fidgeting in her seat and looks extremely uncomfortable. Leaning across to Matthew and Phil, DCS Terry says quietly, "Look, I'm not sure right now is the time to be asking her to do such a thing."

"We've got to ask her sometime. Time is of the essence, you know that. We've got ten days before the seventh of July hits. If we don't find them before that date, I'm certain something bad is going to happen to someone else. Come on, Terry, we've got missing kids that need to come home. This needs to stop now. Whatever message Alice has might be the clue we need. Please, just ask her and see what she says. You know she trusts you," Matthew pleads.

Still unsure, DCS Terry decides to ask the question, "Maria..."

Snapping out of her trance like state, Maria looks up at her once superior and develops a great big smile. "Yes, Terry?"

"We've just been talking, and, you know that the investigation of the missing children is still ongoing, don't you?"

"Yeah."

"You know that the children haven't been found yet..."

"Yeah, I know that."

"Well, we think you might have a really huge part to play in helping us solve this case. What do you think? Would you be able to help us? Would you like to have one more shot at being DC Flores? Show the Force what you're made of."

"Of course," Maria says, grinning from ear to ear. "What do I have to do? Will it help me get out of here so I don't have to look at Derek's ugly mug anymore? If so, I'm in."

Laughing, DCS Terry says, "That's my girl."

"I mean it. He does my head right in."

"Okay – well, don't freak out, just think for a second about what I'm going to say."

"Okay."

"Promise me you're not going to freak out?"

"I promise." Rolling her eyes, she says, "Just spit it out, Terry."

"Well, we were just speaking amongst ourselves and we believe that Alice might be trying to give you some sort of message."

"Right."

"And, we think that message might lead us to the missing children."

"So…"

"So, what we need you to do is find out what the message is."

"How?" Maria's expression has turned fearful. "I can't. Anything but that."

"Calm down, it's okay. Nothing has happened yet. We're just having an adult conversation about it. There's no need to get upset."

"You're going to ask me to stay asleep, aren't you?"

"Maria, don't worry, you'll be fine."

"She would never hurt you, I promise," Phil blurts out. "My Alice hasn't got a bad bone in her body."

Looking unsure, Maria says, "Terry, I don't know, you haven't seen what she looks like. She's not his Alice. I promise you, she's proper dead. You're asking me to hold hands with someone who's dead and looks dead. Her skin is grey. Her throat has a gaping wound on it and she still wears the blood stains down her body. Please don't make me do this. I'll do anything, anything you want, but please, I'm proper scared. I don't want do this."

"Okay, okay, just stay calm. Just hear me out. I've got an idea." DCS Terry decides to try a different approach. "Look, you know me. Ignore everyone else right now and just look directly at me. Can you do that for me?"

"Yes."

"Okay – so, what if you knew we were all in the room next to you?"

"What do you mean?"

"You know me, I've got my fingers in all sorts of pies. What if I could square it so that Matthew, Phil and I would be in the room next to you watching your every move? I'm sure they have rooms in here that have two-way mirrors."

"They do."

"Okay and what about if for extra security we hooked you up to a monitor and if your readings start going erratic, we'll simply wake you up. No biggie."

"You'll wake me up?"

"Yeah – so the machine you'll be hooked to will help us and we'll be able to see if you're getting distressed."

"When would this happen?"

"Well, there's no use in us all just sitting around waiting with you getting even more anxious about it. I mean, what's the time now?" Looking to the watch on his wrist, DCS Terry sees that it is only nine in the morning, "It's only early, I'm certain I could swing it so we could do it tonight. What do you think?"

Maria begins to bounce her legs up and down at a rapid rate, then rocks back and forth, mumbling under her breath.

"Terry, what's she doing?" Phil asks.

"Just shut up a minute, Phil."

DCS Terry is becoming slightly concerned. Maria looks petrified. Desiring nothing more than to get the answers they need, DCS Terry once again speaks, "Maria, I just want to say that you are one heck of a Detective Constable. I'd love nothing more than to work with you again. Here's our one shot. Me and you side by side again."

Maria continues to rock back and forth, her head down, her chin resting on her chest. She doesn't look in DCS Terry's direction.

"Terry, let me try," Matthew says. DCS Terry nods.

"Maria, can you hear me?" Matthew asks.

She doesn't say a word, although her leg stops bouncing.

"I've read multiple articles about how you managed to work your way up the ladder. It's pretty impressive. You went from a job in admin to a high ranked job in the Force and then you continued to work your way right up to the top. You, out of all the admin staff, you were the one that made it. Do you know why?"

Still, Maria says nothing.

"I do. It's because of your passion to get justice for innocent people. I saw the articles on that group of young girls you saved from being sex trafficked. Do you remember that?"

"Yes," Maria says, her voice low.

"Okay, well let's just look at it this way. There are six children who we know are missing. Four boys and two girls. All different ages, but children nonetheless. Let's just imagine they're the same girls. Actually, for a second, let's imagine it's the same case you had all those years ago. Now, ask yourself back then what lengths would you have gone to in order to free those innocent children – what do you think you would have said to yourself?"

"I would have done anything."

"So here's your chance to do that all over again. Here's another group of innocent children who need that strong woman to be brave and go to any lengths to help free them." Standing, Matthew makes his way to the glass and drops to his knees. "Please, I beg you. Please help us free our children. Please, Maria, be brave. You are the only person in the world right now who can potentially help us find them. It's been almost two years since my daughter went missing and almost a year since Phil's children went missing. Please, this might be our only shot at bringing them back home where they belong."

Looking at Matthew, Maria lets out a huge sigh. She slides off her seat, landing on her knees, and waddles her way over to the glass. Kneeling beside the glass, Maria rests her head on it and stares at Matthew.

Putting his hand to the glass, Matthew looks at Maria and smiles. "I know you can do this, Maria. That tough bitch who got you to the top is still in there somewhere. I promise we will be with you every step of the way."

Looking up at Matthew she replies, "But I'm so scared."

"I know you are, Maria. We're all scared. Just think of how scared those children are. All six of them with no mummy or daddy to protect them."

Maria responds, "Okay, I'll do it. But it has to be tonight."

"Really?"

"Yes, I want everything you've promised. I want the room with the two-way mirror that has all of you behind it and I want the monitor so you can wake me up."

"Really?"

"Yes, really."

"Oh my goodness, I cannot thank you enough," Matthew says with a radiant beaming smile upon his face.

Smiling, DCS Terry says, "Consider it done, Maria."

CHAPTER 18

Temimi

It's late afternoon on the twenty-eighth of June. This room in the Moycullen Nunnery is gloomy, uninviting and manifesting a stench of the unholy kind. With no windows, and the door closed tight, the space is suffocating. Hanging from a metal hook is a large lantern. Inside the lantern is an oversized, black candle, with a bright red sinister-looking flame. Thick drops of black wax gradually trickle their way down the sides. The glare from the candle illuminates the room with an intense, disturbing shade of red. There are no pictures on the walls, nor a rug on the floor. Not a single pretty decorative item can be seen. Positioned against the back wall is a dark oak table. Attached to this is an oversized mirror with a chunky dark oak frame. Pushed up against the wall is a wooden bed. The sheets on the bed are black and have been folded with precision. The last item inside the room is a dark oak rocking chair in the corner. On the seat is a bulky black, leather coated, worn looking book. The image on the front of the book is a silver cross, although the cross is not of the pure kind. This deceitful cross is positioned *upside-down*. The chair suddenly *creaks* forwards and *creaks* backwards, completely unaided. There is an unnerving vibration inside the room and the temperature is way below zero. There can only be one explanation for this: evil lives here! The bronze doorknob turns and in walks Sister Jesselle, holding a lantern. Inside the lantern is a white candle. The flame is golden and glowing brightly. Closing the door behind her, Sister Jesselle makes her way to the table. She places the lantern on top of the oak table. There in all its glory, the truth inside this tainted chamber can be seen. Spread randomly across the table are multiple upside-down crosses, engraved deeply in the wood. It appears as though they've been slashed into the wood during a fit of rage. Crosses, all the way down the table legs and surrounding the mirror. It has all been coated. Not a blank space remains. Standing at the table, Sister Jesselle stares at her reflection in the mirror, her head held low. She is empowered by the vision glaring back at her. There she stands in all her glory. No longer Sister Jesselle. No longer her horrific human form, which she cannot bear. No – there stands, her truest form, Jezebel. Proud and ready to take control. Strong and engorged with power. Jezebel is more dangerous than ever. Her red eyes peer out through the gaps in her hair. She's staring at herself intently. Content, she smiles from ear to ear. A thick black substance dribbles from the multiple lacerations on her skin and slowly descends her face. The nauseating element hangs from her chin and drips onto the floor. Oozing from every part of her being, this repulsive liquid has a pungent stench attached to it. Wiping her finger around her mouth, Jezebel collects it and smears an upside-down cross onto the mirror. She throws out her arms in celebration. The candle inside the lantern she brought with her into the chamber turns black and the flame transforms into a deep shade of red. Jezebel's time is coming. Her demonic empire will soon reign. A surge of electricity travels through her veins. Jezebel knows she is unstoppable. No human can match her. No breed upon this planet knows how to take her down. Well, that is except for one and she senses this individual will be soon arriving. Dragging her feet, Jezebel walks across the room towards the rocking chair. Everywhere her feet land, a trail follows. The chair rocks faster and faster. As her final step is taken, the final drag of her grey, wounded foot, the chair miraculously stops. Leaning down, Jezebel collects the black leather book off the chair. Opening the cover, Jezebel suddenly freezes. She senses she's no longer alone. She tilts her head. A sound outside her room has caught her attention. With the book still firmly in her hand, Jezebel closes her eyes and transforms back into her human form. The candle on the wall remains black but the candle on the table returns to its original shade of white and the flame golden. Walking back across to the table, Sister Jesselle places the book down, retrieves the lantern and makes her way to the door. Turning the handle, the door *creaks* as she opens it. Looking dead ahead, Sister Jesselle sees there's no one there. She then steps out of her chamber to inspect further. She turns right and holds her lantern high, shining it down the corridor. Again, she can see no one. Unsure of what it could have been, Sister Jesselle decides to turn around and head back. Making her way back into the room. She closes the door behind her. Only a minute or two passes and then two heavy knocks are heard. Opening the door, she sees Sister Elisabeth kneeling with her head low.

"Ah, Sister Elisabeth, come in."

Sister Elisabeth gets up and walks into the dark and confined space that is Sister Jesselle's chambers. As soon as she enters, Sister Jesselle closes the door and locks it behind her. Without any hesitation, like a trained dog, Sister Elisabeth makes her way to the centre of the room and resumes her kneeling position. Proud of her chosen one, Sister Jesselle makes her way over to the table and places the lantern down. With her back to Sister Elisabeth, she says, "Do you know why I selected you out of all your other Sisters?"

"No," Sister Elisabeth says softly.

Sister Jesselle can hear the anxiety in her voice. It gives her a lusting thrill, "You don't know why I chose to take your soul over theirs?"

"No."

"I chose you because you are the closest sister to the children. The trust they have in you, I needed that to gain quick access to them. You are also easy to manipulate. Each time I entered your dreams it was easy to have you question your faith. As time went by, I knew you were losing your faith. I saw it and so did your Sisters. Would you say you were losing faith?"

"I... was... questioning a few things, yes."

"Questioning the almighty Lord himself. Questioning his ability to save you. Questioning whether or not he was really listening."

"I'd have to agree, Dark Empress."

"Okay – do you see how easy it is for people to lose faith? Your Sisters lost faith in you even though you were trying to warn them that something unholy had entered this building – me. And yet you were still ignored. And then what? You were isolated. You were alone and so what did you do?"

"I surrendered my soul to you."

"The wisest decision you'll have made in your lifetime. Let's see how loyal you really are. Someone is soon to be on their way to the grounds. This person is the only one who has the ability to challenge me. It is imperative that we leave with the children before he reaches the grounds. We need to gain our strength in order to reign fully. Do you understand, Elisabeth?"

"Yes, Dark Empress, I understand."

With her head remaining low, Sister Elisabeth cannot see the transformation taking place before her. Sister Jesselle is no longer Sister Jesselle, she's once again Jezebel. Grabbing the black book from the table, she turns to face Sister Elisabeth.

"Look at me."

Sister Elisabeth does exactly as she's told.

"Now, let me see your true form."

Instantly, a tear falls down Sister Elisabeth's face. But not just any tear. It's black. Sister Elisabeth transforms into a true reflection of her owner. She's no longer Sister Elisabeth, she's an impure entity. She is Elisabeth. Evil now runs through her veins. With eyes that are jet-black, Elisabeth has submitted to the dark side.

Jezebel reaches out her hand and places it underneath Elisabeth's chin.

"Well, well, well, what do we have here? Hmmm, so beautiful. So impure. So new." Placing her nose against Elisabeth's flesh, Jezebel inhales deeply. "I love fresh meat." She then puts her coarse tongue on to the gaping wounds on her face and licks the black substance as it leaves Elisabeth's body. "Let me tell you this: I now own you and if you lose faith in me and if you dare to question my existence then I will torture your soul for all eternity. Do you understand?"

Elisabeth is frozen. Her features are motionless, "Yes, Dark Empress. I understand," she responds in a monotone, deep voice.

Jezebel once again opens the book and begins reciting from one of the pages: "*Intrappolato. Confinato è il tuo spirito. Non più tuo. Con il potere ho preso ciò che è tuo. Mi servi come la tua anima è mia. Temimi. Ti guardo sempre. Dove passo io sarò.*"

Elisabeth's head has dropped and her body has slumped. She has been taken over by the commands.

Empowered by the events taking place before her eyes, Jezebel chants louder and louder, "*Temimi. Temimi. Temimi. Temimi. Temimi!*"

Elisabeth crumples in a heap. Slamming the book closed, Jezebel is content with her possession. She begins dragging herself back to the table and places the book next to the lantern. Looking at her reflection in the mirror, she whispers, "*Temimi.*"

She smiles deceitfully and laughs an insane laugh. Making her way over to the tainted body of Elisabeth on the floor, Jezebel says, "I want the new child. You will help me get to her." Raising her arms, Jezebel commands, "*Salire.*"

Suddenly Elisabeth begins levitating off the ground. Slowly lowering her arms, Elisabeth gradually comes back down to the ground and is now standing in front of Jezebel.

"Return to your human form," Jezebel commands.

The rips in Elisabeth's skin begin absorbing the black substance as they each close one by one. Her skin tone resumes its natural pale shade. Slowly she returns back to Sister Elisabeth. Content with Sister Elisabeth's ability to receive commands and follow them, Jezebel also returns to her human form, "Tonight, you will help me get the new child."

Sister Elisabeth nods.

CHAPTER 19

Sweet Dreams. Sleep Tight

The day has flown by. It's now eight-thirty in the evening and DCS Terry has managed to come through with his promise to Maria. Standing behind the two-way mirror, DCS Terry, Matthew and Phil are all staring as the nurses begin hooking Maria up to the vitals sign monitor.

"Terry, can I have a word over here," Matthew says, pulling DCS Terry to one side.

"Yeah, sure," DCS Terry replies as he follows Matthew to the back of the room.

"Look, Terry, I'm a little concerned."

"It's going to be fine, Matthew, don't worry."

"No, not about this, about something else."

"Huh? What's that, then?"

"Today when we got back to the headquarters, I saw Monty in his car watching us. Without thinking, I went over to the car to confront him. I wanted answers after he almost tried to fuckin' kill me a few days ago."

"Okay. Seems like a valid reaction."

"Well, when I got to the car, it was clear he was hammered. He was shouting at himself and banging his fists on the steering—"

Before Matthew can finish what he's saying, DCS Terry interrupts him, "Look, Matthew, I don't know what you're about

149

to say, but let me just tell you this, you don't need to worry about Lamont," DCS Terry says with a sad expression on his face.

"What do you mean?" Matthew queries.

"Look, I shouldn't tell you this, but he's been admitted to rehab and it seems as though he's gonna be there for a long time. No one knows when he's gonna get out. So seriously, don't worry about him."

"Oh shit."

"Yeah, so let's just focus on why we're here. You ready to rock and roll?"

Taking a deep breath in, Matthew fills his lungs, exhales and says, "No time like the present."

One of the nurses who was attaching the monitor to Maria suddenly enters the room, "DCS Terry, Maria is asking for you. Please follow me."

As he enters the room, he sees Maria looking peaceful on the bed and smiles, "Hey, how are you feeling?"

"I'm okay, Terry. They've given me some relaxers. I don't normally take them because I don't want to sleep, but I figure it might help me to not freak out and might keep me calm so I can help you guys solve this case and bring those children home."

"I think that's a smart move." He tucks her hair behind her ear and DCS Terry continues, "The nurse here said that you wanted to see me."

"Yeah – if I can't wake myself up and you can tell I'm distressed, please, just promise me you'll wake me up."

"I promise. You have my word."

"Okay." Putting out her hand, Maria says, "Will you hold my hand and stay with me until I fall asleep?"

Smiling, DCS Terry replies, "Of course."

The room is quiet. Only the gentle bleeping from the monitors and the tick tock of the clock up high on the wall can be heard. It's almost soothing with its rhythmic tone.

Maria's eyes begin to flicker. She whispers, "I can't stay awake."

"That's good, Maria. It's okay now, you can sleep. I'm here. I promise you will be okay." Rubbing her hands, he says, "Terry's got you."

Maria's eyes flicker for the last time as she gently whispers, "Terry."

Maria is surrounded by the tallest of trees in an unknown forest. The darkness of the night has taken over. Feeling exposed and vulnerable, she stands completely still. The only sound she can hear is that of her breath as it leaves her body. Her heart is pulsating at a rapid rate. Closing her eyes, Maria desperately tries to reassure herself, "Come on, Maria, stay strong."

She feels a chill travel down her spine. She is no longer alone.

"Come on, Maria, be brave," she says, trying to remain calm.

She turns... and sees there's no one there. As she turns back around, she jumps, trips and falls backwards onto the ground, landing up against a tree. Her eyes tell no lies. Standing in front of her is Alice. Her appearance is horrific. There is a great big laceration on her neck and she is covered in bloodstains. Her eyes bulge from their sockets and are dark. Maria breathes deeply to steady herself. All her instincts are telling her to get as far away as she can from the unnatural sight in front of her. Without fully knowing why, she somehow finds the strength to speak.

"You're Alice, right?" she nervously says.

Saying nothing, Alice slightly nods her head just once.

"Can you talk?"

Again, Alice says nothing and slightly shakes her head just the once.

"Do you have something to show me?"

Nodding her head, Alice puts out her hand.

Staring at the horrifying hand which is attached to Alice's lifeless corpse, Maria's stomach turns. She desperately wants to run away, but something stops her. Something about a promise she made.

"You want me to hold your hand?"

Gesturing with her hand once more, Alice nods.

"Okay."

Reluctantly, Maria stands and takes Alice's hand. Instantly, Alice begins guiding Maria at a rapid rate deep into the depths of the eerie forest.

All the nurses, DCS Terry, Matthew and Phil are inside the room behind the mirror. Each one of them is keeping a close eye of Maria's vital signs. Her heart is beating fast – it's erring on the side of dangerous.

"If it goes any higher than this, we're going to have to wake her up," says one of the nurses.

"Agreed," his colleague answers.

"Please just give her some time to adjust, please," Matthew begs.

"I'm sorry, but Maria is my priority, not you. I have to do what's in her best interest," the first nurse tells him.

The nurses look to the machine once more. The numbers begin depleting. Her heartrate and pulse are slowly steading.

"Thank you, God," Matthew says.

Smirking, DCS Terry whispers, "That's my girl."

Alice is leading Maria deeper and deeper into the forest. Something is niggling in Maria's mind. There's something she wants to tell Alice. Suddenly she realises what it is, "Alice, your husband... he's alive."

Alice comes to an abrupt halt. She slowly turns to face Maria. It is apparent by her facial expression, even with her horrific wounded appearance, that she is shocked by this update.

"I'm so sorry, Alice. I shouldn't have said anything, I just thought you should know," Maria says.

The silence is deafening.

"He loves you dearly and is really sorry that he had to leave you all. I know this doesn't make any part of what he did right, but in his eyes Alice, he never left you, he was across the street the whole time," Maria says. "I really shouldn't have said anything, it's really not my place. I just want you to know that Phil is trying to get the children back. You must believe me. He would have never left you if he knew for a second that this would have become your fate. You have to trust me on that one."

Letting go of Maria's hand, Alice stumbles and falls to the ground. Maria isn't sure which way to turn to next. All she wants is to get out of this nightmare she's trapped in. But there's something she needs to do first, something important…

"Alice… do you know where your children are?"

Slowly looking up at Maria, Alice gently nods her head.

"Can you show me? Please?"

Alice remains on the ground.

"This isn't the first time I've seen you. Is that why you keep appearing to me? Because you want to show me where they are?"

Alice continues to stare at Maria.

"Alice, now is your time. I'm here, I'm ready and willing to help you save your babies. I'm so sorry that I upset you. I really am. But please, we have to make this right. We have to save the children. We need to get them back from the monster who took your life and who currently has ownership of theirs. Please, Alice." Still the silence. "Alice, please, just think about this for a second. Why are you doing this? Please, just think back to the reason why you started visiting me. Alice, you know that you're doing this for your children. Those beautiful children who you love so very dearly."

Getting up off the ground, Alice stands still with her head low. She appears to be to be processing the words Maria has just spoken. She holds out her hand and gestures for Maria to hold it once more.

"Thank you," Maria says as she breathes out deeply with great relief.

The pair once again begin running into the depths of the forest. Maria can see lights in the distance radiating from what looks like a huge building. The faster they go, the closer the building gets. Maria is certain that Alice is leading her directly towards it. As they dodge past trees, Maria is continually hit all over her body by stray branches. One hits her with such force in the face that it leaves a very deep scratch on her cheek which begins bleeding. As the pain in her face shocks her, Maria trips and falls on the floor. Moaning out loud, she wipes her cheek. Looking at her hand, she sees bright red blood. She feels a stinging sensation on her cheek and places her hand on it in a desperate bid to soothe the pain. Not wanting to stay in this forest any longer than she has to, Maria quickly wipes her face on her sleeve and puts out her hand to Alice. Alice drags her up off the soil and continues leading Maria towards the building. Eventually, the pair are within meters of the sturdy looking structure.

"What is this place?" Maria questions.

They are standing next to a huge chapel. Standing a few feet away from the chapel is an oversized building with lights glaring through the scattered arched windows. Circulating the whole premises is an elevated steel fence. Alice slowly guides Maria around the fencing. The pair finally reach what appears to be the front entrance. Standing before them are two enormous steel gates. Alice points up high. Looking to where she is pointing, Maria sees arched above the gates in the same steel the words, "Moycullen-Nunnery".

"Is this where they are?"

Alice nods her head. Placing her hand on Maria's face, she pushes her down.

Suddenly, DCS Terry sees Maria open her eyes and throw herself forward. She's soaking wet with sweat from head to toe. He rushes to her bedside, hearing the blaring *bleeps* from the vital signs monitor.

"Maria!" One of the nurses calls out. He lies her back down and strokes her hair, "You're okay. You're safe now. You're back in the room." Looking to his colleague he says, "Quick, get me some sterile wipes. She's got a great big gash on her face. I need to clear it up. This looks deep and I think it might need stiches."

While the nurses busy about, Maria looks directly at DCS Terry, "Terry, she showed me where they are. I know where they are."

Matthew bursts into the room, closely followed by Phil.

"Where?" Matthew says frantically. "Where is my daughter?"

Pushing Matthew back, DCS Terry says, "Calm it, lad."

"It's okay, Terry," Maria says gently.

"What happened?" says Phil quietly from the back of the room.

"Phil, Alice was brave. She held my hand and led me right to where they are."

"And where would that be?" DCS Terry queries.

"It's a place in the darkest forest. You'd never find it alone and you'd never know it exists. Believe me, this forest is not to be messed with. It doesn't appear to be the kind you'd want to get lost in. The children and their captor are living in a building next to a chapel in the forest. It's called Moycullen Nunnery."

Rushing over to Maria, Matthew hugs her. Tears stream down his face, "Thank you." Squeezing her that little bit tighter he says, "Thank you so much for being brave."

"You're welcome," Maria whispers into his ear. "Now go and get your daughter back."

Wiping his face, Matthew steps back and says to Phil, "You ready for this, pal?"

"Are you kidding me? I'd say let's go now, mate." Smiling, Phil makes his way over to Maria's bedside. Touching her arm he says, "So you saw Alice?"

"Yes, I did."

"Did she say anything to you?"

"No, she couldn't speak. She could only gesture."

"Oh."

"I told her that you love her very much."

"She knows I'm alive?"

"Yes. I told her that you're trying your best to get the children back."

Sobbing, Phil says, "I still can't believe I let them all down so much."

"Phil, stop beating yourself up. What's done is done. You cannot rewrite the past but you can adapt the future. You're making it right. Please, just get your children back and raise them with pride. Be the best father you can be. I'm certain Alice will be watching down on you all every day."

"Thank you, Maria."

DCS Terry reaches out to Maria. He hugs her and whispers into her ear, "I knew you could do it." Pulling back, he holds her by her shoulders and says, "Now, you need to get better. You need to do what these people ask of you so that you can come home. I made a promise to you, now I need you to make that promise to me. I don't wanna have to come visit you in here again, okay?"

"Okay."

"Say 'I promise I'll get better and come home, Terry'."

Rolling her eyes and smirking she repeats his words, "I promise I'll get better and come home Terry."

"That's my girl."

Matthew drags DCS Terry to the other side of the room, "So, what do we do now?" he asks. "I'm guessing we find out if this place is real."

"Leave it with me. I'll do some research, try to find the place and see if it even exists. I'm betting it does. I'll get some details and we will take it from there. Just stay calm, at least we've got something to go on. We're almost there."

CHAPTER 20

Kill Her

"Ring a' Ring o' Roses, your souls are mine. Ring a' Ring o' Roses, welcome to the dark side."

After chanting the final, calculated and possessive word, Jezebel raises her hands. In unison, all the children, twenty-six boys and thirty girls, of all different ages, begin to levitate out of their beds. Gasping for air, they are all reacting to the deceitful element that is taking over their DNA. Their physical appearance is transforming at a rapid rate. Their tiny bodies begin to convulse. Jezebel watches through the slight gap in her hair as the children begin jerking back and forth, aware that they are now becoming one with her possessive implantation. As this continues to manifest before her eyes, Jezebel becomes engorged with power. Her beady, deceitful eyes appear illuminated against the darkness within the room. They are turning an intense shade of red. Absorbing each of their souls one by one, Jezebel is receiving their youthful energy and is gaining strength with every submission. A mass collection of life in one swoop. Her plan to rule is aligning. Her empire has multiplied dramatically. With her arms held high, Jezebel shouts, "*Servimi.*"

She then lowers her arms. One by one, each of the children drop from the great height at which they were levitating and land on their beds. Aware that she has full reign over their tiny minds, Jezebel delves deeper to ensure her entrapment is complete. She enters inside each of their bodies through the windows of their souls and sees the evil she has implanted spreading quickly. Latching onto their organs, this uninvited element has created deep roots. Their blood is no longer blue. A thick black substance is surging through the children's veins. No longer pure, no longer conforming to the human race, their hearts are now black. Alongside this inner transformation, the children's physical appearance has also dramatically altered. They're a mirror refection of their new owner, with jet-black hair, dark grey skin and deep lacerations that continually ooze the thick black sinister substance that's rushing around their bodies.

"*Aperta*!" Jezebel commands.

In perfect synchronisation, the children's eyelids shoot open. No longer blue, green, hazel or brown, their eyes have transformed and are jet-black. The whites in their eyes can no longer be seen. The thick black substance drips from the surrounding gaps on their eye sockets. Standing by the doorway, showcasing their true horrific demonic forms, are Eve, Lewis, Freddie, Terence and Rupert. Appearing to be pleased with their new arrivals, they are smirking with their heads held low as they stand patiently. Getting ready to give her orders, Jezebel looks to her evil accomplices. She sees Eve licking her lips. Getting a huge thrill from watching Eve's reaction, Jezebel locks eyes with her and then twitches her head. With a giant sneer upon her face, Jezebel says, "It is almost time, my child. Be patient." She then looks at Lewis. Confused, she asks, "Where is the baby?"

Saying nothing, Lewis looks to Eve and then puts his head down.

"Sleeping. She is of no use to you right now," Eve says.

Jezebel hears a dulcet giggle coming from the back of the room. She turns her head in the direction where the childlike sound came from and grins once more. The room is gloomy, since night has begun to take over, but this doesn't prevent Jezebel from spotting her youngest addition to her empire. Enthused by Hope's quick ability to embrace the evil within her, Jezebel proudly observes the results. Loaded with egotistical gratification, Jezebel oversees every one of Hope's movements. Hope is up high on the wall in her demonic form.

Placing one hand and one leg in front of the other, Hope is crawling her way around the wall, defying the laws of gravity. She seems to be in her element as she scurries around, giggling and mumbling away to herself. Jezebel is satisfied that the evil she has implanted within this child is of great strength. Aware she would need more than the human body to carry out her universal takeover, Jezebel has laced each of her accomplices with an inimitable ability.

"Let this be a message to you all. I have given you power outside of anything mankind could possibly offer you. Stay loyal to me and remain under my command and you will live an extraordinary existence," Jezebel announces. Pointing in Hope's direction she shouts, "Look, look at what each of you can become."

All eyes in the room are on Hope. Everyone is watching as she fearlessly picks up speed. Wherever Hope travels, a trail of the thick black substance can be seen following her, smearing across the walls. Hope starts to giggle as she notices the black substance. Suddenly Hope stops and begins squishing the substance through her fingers in a playful manner.

"Come here, my baby," Jezebel calls.

Without hesitation, Hope scurries across the walls towards Jezebel. She then dashes down onto the floor and in between the children's beds, placing herself at the side of her owner. Putting out her arms, Hope gestures to be picked up. Collecting Hope from off the floor, Jezebel smiles as she cradles her. Dragging one foot after the other, she then begins to make her way around the room.

Jezebel makes eye contact with Eve and twitches her head, "Collect their substance. Check their souls. Ensure every one of them has surrendered to my empire."

Eve then looks to Lewis, Freddie, Terence and Rupert and relays the orders Jezebel has just given, "We have been commanded. We must collect each of their substances and ingest it to taste the poison. Gaze through their eyes, which are the windows of the soul, to check that they no longer have ownership of their souls. We then have to ensure that every one of them has surrendered to our Dark Empress's empire. When you have done this, you command *Temimi*. Do you understand?"

In unison they respond, "Yes."

"Now go."

Jezebel watches as her plan finally comes together. Doing exactly as they have been commanded, her evil accomplices are spreading out to solidify her possessive entrapment. Heading to the closest bed, Eve reaches out and collects the black substance from a boy who is no more than eight years of age. She puts her finger to her mouth and begins ingesting it. Smiling and appearing content with its bitter taste, Eve then places her hand against the boy's face, leans over and stares intently at his eyes. She then commands, "*Temimi.*"

Lewis, Freddie, Terence and Rupert are all completing this process. Programmed by Jezebel, not a single one of them hesitates as they make their way to the next child and then the next child. Jezebel is satisfied that the children will remain under her control and be accepted into her dark universe. She's basking in the glory of the image that lies before her. Her time is coming. Soon she will reign and soon she will be free.

Jezebel shouts, "Now you belong to me, the Dark Empress. You are under my control, you live within my empire, my universe, and you will serve at my feet. If any of you defy me, you will die."

Before she can continue, Jezebel is suddenly knocked off course as she notices one of the little girls sit upright in her bed. Peering across the room, Jezebel realises it's young Rita. A child she is familiar with due to her immediate tolerance and absorption of her possessive entrapment. With her back straight and her head low, Rita opens her mouth. The thick black substance gushes down her chin. With a distorted and deep voice, she says, "Dark Empress."

Dragging her feet, Jezebel makes her way towards Rita's bed, "Eve, come get the child," she calls holding out baby Hope.

Without hesitation, Eve makes her way to Jezebel, takes Hope from out of her arms and stands directly by Jezebel's side. Leaning across to Rita, Jezebel places her hand underneath her chin. Staring deep into her eyes, Jezebel sees Rita has fully submitted herself to the dark side. Pleased with her progress, Jezebel says, "Yes, child."

"I am ready. Complete me."

No sooner has Rita spoken these words than the sound of jingling keys can be heard coming from the corridor outside the room. One of the sisters is on her way to conduct the night-time check on the children.

Aware this is an opportunity to see just how far her new addition will go, Jezebel whispers in Rita's ear, "*Uccidila.*"

Staying sat upright in her bed, Rita doesn't move an inch. Now the sound of jingling keys is getting closer and a small light can be seen flickering in the corridor through the gaps around the door.

Raising her arms, Jezebel commands the rest of the room, "*Essere ancora.*"

As soon as the order is given, the rest of the children are restrained and lay stiff inside their beds. Jezebel, along with Eve, who is cradling Hope, Lewis, Freddie, Terence and Rupert all disappear into the darkest depths of one of the corners in the room. They are not visible to the human eye.

Sister Marie pushes the creaking door to the children's dorm room open and goes inside. She scans the room. At first glance all seems as it should be. But soon enough something catches her attention. One of the children is sat up in their bed, "My dear child, you gave me a fright," she says quietly as she heads towards the child's bedside.

Getting closer, Sister Marie soon works out that it is Rita. Without a reaction or a word from Rita, Sister Marie assumes she is dreaming. Placing her hand on Rita's shoulder Sister Marie attempts to lay her back down on her bed. However, Rita doesn't move an inch. Feeling her stiff body and fast becoming confused, Sister Marie says, "Rita darling, is everything okay?"

No response.

"Darling, why don't you lay yourself back down? You can't sleep like that all night." Again, not so much as a flinch comes from Rita, nor does she speak. Aware something isn't right, Sister Marie leans into Rita's ear and nervously says, "Rita?"

Without moving her body, Rita slowly turns her head one hundred and eighty degrees and stares at Sister Marie. Gasping at

Rita's inhumane ability and the horrific sight before her eyes, Sister Marie realises that there is something unholy inside this child. She panics. Dropping the lantern on the floor, she frantically tries to grip the cross attached to the rosary beads hanging around her neck. Before her fingers can find the cross, Rita jumps up at her. She feels a sharp stabbing pain. Rita has latched on to her skin and is biting through her neck. Sister Marie screams out, desperate to raise the alarm, "Help! Dear God, please, somebody help me!"

The door *slams* shut and the lock clicks. With no hope of rescue, Sister Marie tries to free herself, pushing her fingertips into Rita's face. Unfortunately for her, Rita doesn't move an inch and continues gorging her way through her flesh. Powerless, Sister Marie continues screaming and crying out, "Help me, please, somebody!"

Overseeing the savage attack, Jezebel appears from out of the distance, dragging one foot in front of the other. She touches each child she passes and says, "*Scia.*"

Getting up from their beds, they follow Jezebel as she makes her way towards Rita. Reaching the middle of the room where Rita is devouring her victim, Jezebel commands the ten children she has woken up: "*Uccidila.*"

Without hesitation, they join Rita and attach themselves to Sister Marie's body. Soon enough, Sister Marie's pleas stop. The only sound that can be heard is the flesh being ripped from her body.

Satisfied, Jezebel commands, "*Abbastanza.*"

The children scatter back to their beds. Kneeling at the side of Sister Marie's severely wounded deceased body, Jezebel places her finger on her neck. She gathers some of the blood gushing from the gaping wound and ingests it.

"Mmmm, so warm."

Jezebel smiles at Rita, who is sat on the edge of her bed with blood smeared around her mouth. Placing her hand on Rita's head, Jezebel says, "Well done, my child. Patience has been a virtue. Our time is coming."

CHAPTER 21

I will not let you down

Under Jezebel's command and on a different mission, Sister Elisabeth enters Sister Eve's bedroom. Closing the door behind her and locking it, Sister Elisabeth places her lantern on the bedside table and makes her way across to the white wooden crib where four-month-old baby Honey is sleeping. Peering inside the crib, Sister Elisabeth sees Honey is lay flat on her back and is tucked tightly into her white cotton bedsheets. She is blissfully sleeping and has not moved an inch. Just above Honey's head there is a silver cross dangling from some wooden rosary beads. Smiling, Sister Elisabeth whispers, "Huh, so pure."

Stepping back, Sister Elisabeth starts to transform. She is embracing the transition and gaining pleasure from the gashes which are now ripping their way through her flesh. No longer human, this evil version of her is engulfed with power. Standing in her true horrific form, Elisabeth has her head low. She slowly drags one foot in front of the other and is making her way back to Honey's crib. Black liquid is trailing behind her. Arriving at the side of the crib, Elisabeth opens her mouth and the black liquid begins gushing down her chin as she whispers, "I am here for you. It is now your time to join the dark side. Ring a' Ring o' Roses…"

As she is singing her possessive rhyme, Elisabeth leans into the crib and attempts to collect Honey. As soon as her hands graze

Honey's bedsheets, an unforeseen force surrounds this precious baby girl and Elisabeth is thrown across the room. Banging her head against the wall, Elisabeth is instantly knocked unconscious. Lay on the floor, her body quickly returns back to her human form and she is once again Sister Elisabeth.

Around ten minutes pass, Sister Elisabeth moans as she gently begins to arouse herself. Bringing her hand to the back of her head, Sister Elisabeth touches this tender area and scrunches her face as she feels a surge of excruciating pain. With her fingers moist, she looks to her hand and sees bright red blood. Standing, Sister Elisabeth stumbles slightly. Holding onto Sister Eve's bedframe, she gathers her bearings as she again makes her way across to Honey's crib. Peering over the side, she sees Honey is still sleeping and again has not moved an inch. Believing she conducted the possession incorrectly, Sister Elisabeth grabs the lantern and rushes out of the room in a panic. She has no idea how she is going to explain to Sister Jesselle that she has failed.

CHAPTER 22

So Close

The clock is ticking. Almost forty-eight hours have passed since Sister Alannah ventured into the forest alone with Brennan. It's mid-afternoon and Sister Alannah is battling against the branches that are hitting her in the face. Having left the outdoor chapel in a hurry, she is desperate to flee the chapel and return to the nunnery without getting caught. Nervous, she's continually checking over her shoulder to ensure that no one is following her as she strides through the overgrown grass. Fast becoming out of breath, Sister Alannah has allowed her emotions to take control of her thoughts. Fear is circulating throughout her body. With the repercussions of her actions at the forefront of her mind, Sister Alannah's aware that her loyalty at this present moment is lying outside of her convent and this may come at a huge price. Not caring, she continues with her mission as she follows her heart. Tripping over the twigs and stones concealed by the grass, she twists her ankle as she stumbles slightly. Hobbling, Sister Alannah starts to pant as her lungs become tight and her throat dries up. Finally reaching the gates, she slides through the slight gap to prevent the hinges from creaking. She's desperate not to draw attention to herself. Completing this successfully, Sister Alannah staggers her way towards the giant wooden arched door. As she pushes it open, her heart is beating faster than ever. Closing the door behind her, she frantically heads for the staircase. No longer caring about the pain in her ankle, she holds up the multiple layers of material under her skirt to prevent herself from tripping again. With a one-track mind, she begins leaping up the staircase two steps at a time. Arriving at the bedroom door, Sister Alannah stands for a moment and inhales deeply. Regaining control of her breath, she slowly turns the handle and opens the door.

"Brennan," she quietly says as she peers into the room. "Brennan, are you awake?"

Seeing that his body doesn't move, Sister Alannah creeps through the doorway. She then closes the door behind her. Anxious about the outcome, she presses her hand and her head against the frame of the door. She's worried and doesn't really know what to do. Now realizing the lengths she's about to go to for lust or love, Sister Alannah feels a small amount of guilt at the betrayal she's about to commit against not only her sisters but her longstanding beliefs. Breathing deeply once more, gathering her thoughts, Sister Alannah starts to weigh up the pros and cons in her head. Questioning herself, she's wondering about the severity of her current actions and how this could possibly end. Closing her eyes, she considers the thought of leaving the nunnery and never being able to return. And yet if she chooses to stay, and gives Brennan the opportunity to leave, she knows as soon as her sisters find out what she's done, they will put her in segregation. Facing the possibility of being ostracized like Sister Elisabeth, Sister Alannah doesn't want to take the risk. She'd rather leave with the boy she's grown fond of than be locked away by her fellow sisters. Making her final decision, Sister Alannah is adamant she is going through with her initial plan. Turning, she sees Brennan is sleeping peacefully in his bed. She can tell he is unaware of her presence as he hasn't even flinched. Making her way to his bedside, she places her hand on his shoulder and shakes him slightly, "Brennan, you need to wake up."

In a daze, Brennan replies, "Huh." Adjusting his sight, he sees Sister Alannah leaning over him. "What's wrong?"

"You need to wake up. Sister Marie has gone missing and no one can find her. Sister Briana is suggesting that you might have something to do with this."

Rubbing his eyes and yawning, Brennan says, "What did you just say?"

"Brennan, please, I need you to wake up. Sister Marie has gone missing. No one has seen her or can find her anywhere."

"Okay, hey, calm down, it's going to be okay. She's probably gone for a walk."

"No, Brennan, you don't understand, Sister Briana is trying to blame you for her disappearance."

"What? Me? Is she out of her mind?"

Aware that she's about to take the biggest leap in her life for someone she has known for only a few days, Sister Alannah decides she has to ask the question, "Brennan, please, be honest, do you have any idea where she might have gone?"

"No – are you joking? Of course I don't where she is. Why would you even ask me that?" Appearing offended at the suggestion, Brennan throws back the covers and gets out of the bed. "I mean, it's not rocket science. Think about it logically, do you even know how long she has been missing?"

Sister Alannah blushes as she sees him standing in front of her wearing nothing but his underwear. She can see the outline of his penis which is hanging loosely inside his boxer shorts. Her eyes widen. She turns her head, trying not to become distracted.

Continuing to blush, Sister Alannah doesn't look Brennan's way as she speaks, "Erm, Sister Marie was supposed to be conducting the late-night check on the children. Sister Cathleen said she saw her leaving her room to head to the children's room. She then said that Sister Marie had mentioned that she wasn't feeling too great. When she knew the next check was due to take place, Sister Cathleen went to Sister Marie's room to tell her that she would conduct the check to allow her to rest and when she got there, Sister Marie wasn't there. She said her light wasn't on either and it didn't look as though she'd been back to her room."

"So, maybe she fell asleep with one of the children."

"That's what she thought. Well, she thought that Sister Marie might have passed out in the children's room because she looked so poorly. So Sister Cathleen then went to the children's room and Sister

Marie wasn't there either. First thing this morning she went back to Sister Marie's room because she was still concerned, and again she was nowhere to be seen and the room was in the exact same condition it was when she visited it a few hours earlier. She again went back to the children's room and Sister Marie wasn't there either. Sister Cathleen then checked the nunnery, the chapel and asked the other sisters if they'd seen or heard from her and they all confirmed that they hadn't."

"Right, well maybe she left."

"No, this is Sister Marie, she would never leave. She's a loyal sister and has been here for in excess of thirty years. She would never abandon her sisters, the children or the nunnery."

"Okay, but I don't understand what this has got to do with me, I was with you all last night, you can vouch for me surely?"

"No – I can't. The last time Sister Marie was seen, it was around one in the morning and I was back inside my room way before then."

"Sister Alannah, you don't think I had anything to do with this, do you?" Brennan says as he makes his way across the room towards her.

As he reaches out and touches her arm, Sister Alannah looks him straight in his eyes. Seeing the sincerity in his features, Sister Alannah knows this wasn't him, how could it be with those great big brown puppy dog eyes, "I don't believe it was you, but my sisters are very suspicious. Sister Briana is gunning for you. She's convincing everyone right now that you had something to do with this and that they should all ambush you and have you locked away before another one of our sisters goes missing."

"Are you being serious? Ambush me? For what? I haven't even done anything. Well, let them ambush me because I have nothing to hide so I'm going nowhere. Us New Yorkers stand strong. We don't shy away."

"Brennan, this is serious, I think we should leave."

"Leave?" he says. "Wait, we?"

"Yes, I can't possibly belong here anymore now that you have arrived. I cannot continue to preserve my life to the Lord because

I no longer have love in my heart for him alone. This goes against everything I have committed to throughout my life."

Shocked, Brennan replies, "Wow, I'm flattered." Smiling, he continues, "Well, when do you want to go?"

"*Now*. I think we should leave now. Pack your things."

"Really, Sister Alannah, are you sure this is what you want? I will stay here with you."

"Brennan, you do not understand what some of these sisters are capable of. You will not survive, they will make sure of it. All those people who were lost in the forest and never found – do you really believe it was because of the spirit world? Because I can tell you now, it was not. Some of my sisters will do anything to try to preserve the sacredness of our home. And yet all that has happened is darkness has followed."

Removing her habit and veil, Sister Alannah drops the items on the floor and steps out of the layers of material she's wearing. Standing in a pair of thin black trousers and a black long-sleeved top, Sister Alannah says, "I'm no longer Sister Alannah. My heart belongs to you. From now on, I am Alannah."

Gazing at her, Brennan reaches over and tucks her hair behind her ear. He then says, "I've been waiting to do this for ages," as he leans in for a kiss.

Feeling his soft plump lips on hers, Alannah runs her fingers through his hair. She's never felt excitement and passion like this before in her life. The thrill is addictive and she's getting a rush of adrenaline surging around her body. Pulling back, she smiles as her mind becomes fuzzy.

"It's going to be okay," Brennan whispers.

Zoning back into the room, Alannah says, "Brennan, you need to get dressed quickly, and collect your things, we must leave now, we've got limited time. I think everyone is still in the chapel but I cannot be certain so we must sneak out quietly."

"Okay," Brennan says as he grabs his clothes off the chair and begins getting dressed.

Watching him dress, Alannah is admiring the view.

Throwing his jacket on, he then places his backpack over his shoulders and says, "Okay, I'm ready. Wait, what about your clothes?"

Laughing under her breath at his innocence, Alannah says, "Brennan, we do not have materialistic items such as clothes here at the nunnery. I have only the black outfit which I am standing in now and that's it."

"Wow, that's crazy. I couldn't imagine not having a wardrobe full of the clothes."

Gazing at him in admiration, unable to fight the urge, slightly aroused, Alannah grabs Brennan and kisses him passionately. She places her forehead onto his and they both smile. The madness of what she's about to do starts sinking in and she's thriving from it.

"We must be quick but quiet. Do you understand?"

"Yes."

Leaving the safety of the room, Alannah and Brennan begin making their way down the corridor. Reaching the top of the staircase the pair are almost free. Suddenly Brennan shouts out, "Argh!" and jumps.

Turning, the pair see Sister Elisabeth standing behind them.

"Going somewhere you two?" Looking at Sister Alannah's current attire, she comments, "Sister Alannah, you look inappropriately dressed." Smirking, she continues, "Hm, what exactly is going on here?"

Pushing Brennan behind her, Alannah says, "I was just leading Brennan out of the Forest so he can find his way home."

"Why do I get a distinct feeling that you are lying to me?"

"I'm not, why would I lie to you?"

Scowling at the pair, Sister Elisabeth says, "Hmm, well, make sure you return soon, Sister Alannah." Sister Elisabeth then gently rolls her eyes, shakes her head and continues making her way down the corridor.

"That was so close," Alannah says as she looks at Brennan with great relief, "Come on." She grabs his arm and begins dragging him down the staircase.

Opening the door, Alannah lets Brennan out first. She then turns and takes one final glance at the nunnery.

Taking a deep breath in she says, "Goodbye, Father, goodbye sisters, goodbye children. I will think about you always and I will love you forever."

"Alannah, what are you doing? Come on, we've got to go."

Smiling one last time, she closes the door behind her and says, "I'm coming."

The pair run through the gates and do not look back.

CHAPTER 23

The Day of Reckoning Has Arrived

Sat inside Matthew's dining room are Matthew, Phil and DCS Terry. They have their heads bent over a map, planning the best way to forge through the forest to reach their destination. Since Maria's findings last night, they have conducted lengthy research and now know the exact location of the Moycullen Forest and the Nunnery. They have read multiple articles about this peculiar and intimidating location and watched hours of footage online, which has repeatedly warned them about the dangers of entering this forest. Matthew, Phil and DCS Terry have each watched videos of people inside the forest and every single one of them have freaked out at various supernatural findings. Some of the clips are from cameras that have been found by explorers as they walked through the forest. This footage has to be the eeriest as it reveals the identity of individuals who were last seen venturing into the forest and have not been seen since. And yet, in all the hours of footage they have seen, not a single one has shown the nunnery. It is described as unholy by all those who have blogged about and recorded in this location. What's even more concerning is that each of them share the same view and it is not a positive one. Not allowing this to frighten him, Matthew scans the map with intensity. His mind is racing as he desperately tries to work out the best approach to get inside the nunnery undetected.

"What time is the flight booked?" he asks.

Looking to his watch, DCS Terry says, "It leaves at four-forty-six. We've got around three hours. We're going to have to leave soon as we need to be at the airport within the next hour."

"How are we really going to get into this place?" Phil says nervously.

"I think the best bet is to get there and just charge at it." Matthew says.

"But what about the stuff we've found online?"

"Phil, seriously, it's just a bunch of ghost stories, probably to try to encourage tourism. Look at it this way: we're living in a real-life nightmare that is way worse than anything those people have described. Come on, pull yourself together. We're so close to getting our children back. If they're really in there, you could be cuddling your babies by the end of the day. How does that sound?" Matthew says.

"Yeah, that does sound nice," Phil responds, smiling.

"Okay, so pull yourself together, we've got this mate."

Afternoon prayer inside the outdoor chapel has now come to an end. All of the sisters are heading back to the nunnery with the children. Walking in single sex order, there is a row of boys, a row of girls and the sisters are spread out in the middle guiding the children. The walk is not a long one; however, it is long enough for the children to get into all sorts of mischief should they not be supervised. The grass has grown and has masked part of the pathway, leaving each of them to grapple their way through. With a bang and a grumble, the sky suddenly becomes overcast. It almost appears as if a huge thunderstorm is about to hit. Leading the way, Sisters Kathryn, Cathleen, Briana and Jennifer are marching quickly back to the nunnery. As they walk, Sister Briana doesn't notice the change in weather as she cannot rest her mind. She is concerned about their newest arrival and the disappearance of Sister Marie and so she questions Sister Kathryn about Sister Alannah's disappearance the other night, "Sister, I know you know something. I can see it in your eyes."

Saying nothing, Sister Kathryn puts her head down.

"Tell me what you know. It's the American boy, isn't it?"

Still saying nothing, Sister Kathryn looks over her shoulder.

"What are you hiding, Sister?" Sister Briana says. She stops in her tracks and pulls on Sister Kathryn's arm.

Turning to Sister Cathleen, Sister Kathryn says, "Please continue to take the children back to the nunnery. I just need to speak with Sister Briana."

Nodding her head, Sister Cathleen says, "Okay, children, be careful now, follow me and Sister Jennifer."

"Is everything okay?" Sister Jennifer says, stopping at Sister Kathryn's side.

"Yes. Just go back to the nunnery with your sisters and the children. Please prep the children and have them ready for their dinner," Sister Kathryn replies.

"Of course. Please just let me know if there is anything else I can do."

"Thank you."

Sister Kathryn pulls Sister Briana's arm "We cannot speak here, follow me." She leads her behind one of the trees for privacy, then continues, "You cannot repeat this. I do not want the sisters or the children to find out and get scared."

"I promise."

"A few weeks ago I became aware of something unholy within our walls. I went to the chapel and asked for our Father to show me what it is. I asked our Father to allow me to see the evil that is trying to taint our precious home. He granted me this. Sister, it is not the American boy. He is just a boy. This is something malevolent on a higher frequency. The evil that is running through our precious home is strong."

"What... erm... what do we do?"

"I've been praying every night, trying to get answers, to find out how we can defeat this evil. As I hear it and feel it, there is only one person who can save our souls. If this person doesn't make it in time, we will all die."

"What do you mean? Can we not just leave? Sister, surely there's a way to escape this."

"Sister, there is no way to escape fate, we both know that."

"Why on earth haven't you been trying to plan something? I don't know, maybe try to locate a refuge that we can go to."

"Sister, we cannot leave the grounds we have committed our lives to. It would be the biggest of sins. This is our home. I've been praying and asking for clarity. Today I received a message from our Father. He told me that the person we need is soon to be here. I keep praying every chance I get that this person will be guided here before it's too late. Have faith, Sister. Whatever is meant for us will be."

"Why is evil here? What does it want?"

Sister Kathryn pauses. She has a look of sorrow on her face as she quietly says, "The children."

Just as the words leave her mouth, an almighty toe-curling scream echoes through the forest. It's coming from the nunnery. This shriek is followed by the cries of many. Turning, the pair instantly lift their skirts and run through the grounds of the chapel. As the nunnery comes into sight, Sister Kathryn can see the children crying in the front yard and the sisters attempting to console them. Frantic, the pair run through the crowd. Making her way to Sister Cathleen, Sister Kathryn says, "What's happened?"

Appearing traumatised, Sister Cathleen doesn't say a word. Her hand is shaking as she points to the doorway.

Looking to Sister Briana, Sister Kathryn says, "Stay here."

Without hesitation, Sister Briana responds, "Not a chance. If you're going in there, Sister, then so am I. There's no way I am leaving you alone with this thing."

The pair walk hand in hand towards the doorway, breathing deeply. They push the door open and its hinges creak as it slowly swings. As Sister Kathryn takes a step inside, her nose is hit by a pungent stench. Letting go of Sister Briana's hand, she covers her nose and takes a further step inside. She looks up high and is confronted with a sickening sight. Her stomach cramps and she throws up on the floor. Sister Briana peers through the doorway. She sees exactly what Sister Kathryn has seen. Falling backwards, Sister Briana slumps against the wall outside and falls to the floor. Gathering her thoughts, Sister Kathryn wipes her mouth and steps outside of the nunnery. Peering across to Sister Briana, she says, "Please, stay outside, Sister. I will be fine. Our Father will protect me." Sister Kathryn then bravely goes inside and closes the door behind her.

Catching her breath and trying to regain control of her thoughts, Sister Kathryn prays for her stomach to stop turning, "Come on, you can do this."

She looks up once more and tears stream from her eyes. The sight is too traumatising to ignore. Falling to her knees, she places her hand around her stomach, desperately trying to stop the gut-wrenching pain she's feeling. Her thoughts are racing at what feels like a hundred miles per hour.

"Please, Father, say this isn't true. Please."

The stench circulating in the air is becoming stronger with every second that passes. Feeling the support from her Father, Sister Kathryn is determined to conquer her fears and remove the evil that has intruded into her home before anyone else gets hurt. With this at the forefront of her mind, she bravely shouts, "Why, did you do this? Show yourself."

There is a deafening silence.

"You can't have them. They are not yours to take," she shouts.

Still she gets no response. The only sound she can hear is her own voice. Staring at the catastrophic image before her eyes, Sister Kathryn cries out loud. Her wails echo throughout the nunnery. Tears stream from her eyes, blurring her vision.

Above her, six bodies hang from the top of the staircase. They have been stripped of their clothes and dangle naked from thick, coarse ropes. The corpses are covered in blood and directly below each one is a puddle of thick red blood. The vision is horrific. Sister Marie, Mark and four other male bodies, all of whom are members of the kitchen staff, are hanging from the great height looking like rag dolls, not human bodies that once housed a soul. They mustn't have stood a chance against the evil within the walls. Firmly holding her cross in her hand, Sister Kathryn scans the area. Her eyes are instantly drawn to a smearing of blood on one of the walls which reads 'They are not yours to keep'. Closing her eyes, Sister Kathryn breathes deep as the surge of vomit is desperately trying to escape her body. The stench is becoming more and more unbearable by the second. Scanning the area once more, seeing no one, she says, "You cannot hide from me. Show yourself."

All she can hear is the echoing and her voice. Lifting herself off the floor, she begins making her way up the staircase. About halfway up, she hears a distant scratching sound and stops. She turns and sees there's no one there. A cold chill graces her skin and travels down her neck. She feels a presence behind her, and it isn't of the pure kind. But before she has time to process this, a scratching noise comes from the direction of the doorway she has just walked through. Sister Kathryn isn't sure if she should run up the stairs or back down towards the door. Before she has time to make her decision, the door handle begins to bounce up and down, as though someone on the outside is frantically trying to get inside. The knocker bangs aggressively and she hears screaming. Believing it is her fellow sisters and the children trying to get back inside the nunnery, Sister Kathryn runs down the staircase and straight towards the door.

Sitting in the back of the taxi, Matthew is gearing himself up for the challenge that lies ahead. His heart is pounding, his palms are becoming sweaty and his mind is racing. His inner voice taunts him.

Ha, she's not even going to be there, you dumb ass. Travelling all this way because some crazy lady said she had a dream. She's just as nuts as you are.

Wanting the incessant voice to be quiet, Matthew whispers, "Shut up."

Crazy Matthew at it again. Even if you do find your daughter, do you really think she's going to come home with you? You, really? The guy who lost it all. Seriously, what do you even have to offer her except an alcohol addiction?

The relentless internal voice begins laughing insanely. Matthew can't take it anymore. Smacking himself in the head, he shouts, "Just shut up, damn it!"

"Matty lad, are you okay?" says DCS Terry from the other side of the taxi.

Slowly, Matthew begins rocking back and forth.

Phil is sitting directly next to Matthew. He reaches out and holds Matthew by the arm, "Mate, it's going to be okay. Just look at me. Stop panicking, because you're going to give yourself an anxiety attack. Just look at me and breathe."

Staring directly into Phil's eyes, Matthew calms slightly as he breathes deeply.

"That's it, mate. Just stay focused on me and keep breathing deeply. It's all good. We're just going to get our children back, that's all. Think of it as we're picking them up from a camping trip. No biggie, mate."

"We've got this, lads," DCS Terry chips in, "Come on, we're so close."

"Believe me, I'm ready," Matthew says as he looks at his hands, which are beginning to tremble, "I'm just anxious. Each time I've gotten so close. It's just frustrating. And now I question whether my daughter even wants to be saved. What if she takes one look at me and says no thank you?"

"Matthew, you must stop it. You're no good to her like this. Your daughter loves you and I'm sure she'll be happy to see you. Come on, mate, don't let the voices in your head win this round. We're so close," Phil says.

"You're right. God, why is anxiety such a bitch? It always gets me at the times I need it the least."

With a sincere smile, Phil says, "Matthew, I'm scared, too. It's okay. We've got each other's backs. You're not alone in this anymore. The end is in sight. We're going to get our children and bring them home."

"Phil, I just pray we're not too late if they are here. Look at the sky, don't you think it's all too familiar?"

"Mate, it's okay, we won't be too late, ignore the sky and have faith."

Aware they're not far from their destination, Matthew sits in silence. He's looking out of the window at the sky and twiddles his fingers to try to distract himself from his anxiety.

"Do you both remember what we're going to do?" DCS Terry asks.

"Sorry, can you just go over it again, Terry? I'm a little nervous myself mate and don't want to mess it up," Phil says.

"It is important that we stay close to one another while we are making our way through the forest. Do not wander off at any point. Look, I've got the map of the forest here." Taking a piece of paper out of his pocket, DCS Terry unfolds it and points to a red cross. "This is where the taxi is taking us. We're then going to head this way for around fifteen minutes, we should then be approaching the back of the nunnery. Once we get to this spot, we're going to scan the perimeter. As discussed, so we've got eyes everywhere, Matthew, you will stay at the back of the nunnery here to make sure she doesn't sneak out with the children. Phil, you will be at the chapel entrance way over here. I need you to try to get a look inside to see whether they're in there or not. And I will make my way to the front entrance as agreed. I will knock at the door to see if I can get someone to answer. They haven't seen my face before so I am the least suspect should Jezebel, Eve or any of Phil's children answer the door. Have you each got your radio?"

Waving his in the air, Phil says, "Yep."

"Yes," Matthew says.

The taxi journey from the airport to the Moycullen Forest seems longer in time than it has taken. They arrive at the forest by their chosen entrance. Matthew steps out of the taxi, closely followed by Phil and DCS Terry. Standing by the side of the road, Matthew takes a deep breath. Looking to Phil and DCS Terry, he exhales heavily, blowing his anxiety away. Matthew is ready to face the unknown.

Looking up at the sky, he shakes his head, "Oh no, no, no, no, no, no, this isn't good."

"Huh?" Phil says with confusion fast spreading across his face.

"We need to hurry." Matthew points to the sky. "Something terrible is about to happen. Those clouds turning from grey to black and joining like that are never a good sign. Terry, quick what's the entrance plan?"

"I think we should go this way," Terry says as he is pointing to the sheet of paper that has the planned-out map on it. He then points to the entrance and says, "It bends round to the right there." Looking to Matthew and Phil, DCS Terry says, "So, it's now or never, lads. Are you ready to see if we can get your children back and finally get justice for all those who have suffered?"

"As ready as I'll ever be," Phil says.

With a gentle smile, Matthew says, "You know it, Terry."

Matthew's heartrate gradually begins to pick up speed as he follows DCS Terry into the forest. Breathing deeply, he tries to stay in control of his anxiety levels. They are surrounded by trees that stand strong, one after the other. These overgrown contributions to the planet are intimidating. There are hundreds of trees with thick branches and oversized leaves. Like a blanket, the leaves block out the natural daylight and the forest has an eerie, unnatural darkness. Matthew trips and lands in a pile of mud, "Shit, that's disgusting," he says as he begins wiping his hands on his trousers.

"Mate, are you okay?" Phil says as he pulls Matthew up off the ground.

"Yeah. I just tripped over that massive tree root. Look at the size of that," he says, pointing. Matthew becomes confused as something catches his eye behind the tree root. A tiny pink grubby teddy bear's foot peeps out of the ground. Matthew digs it out and cleans it off. His jaw drops as he realises what it is. Turning, he says to Phil, "Look at this."

Phil snatches it out of his hand, "Where did you get this from?"

"It was buried just over there. Phil, is this what I think it is?"

"Yeah," Phil says as he breaks down crying.

"Excuse me, lads, am I missing something here?" DCS Terry says.

"Phil got this bear for his unborn daughter before he left. It's got her name sewn into the stomach."

"Let me see that," DCS Terry says as he takes it out of Phil's hands. "Well, this is a good thing. At least we know we're on the right track and Maria was correct. This should motivate you even more."

"I suppose it has just shocked me. I didn't think I'd see this again. The last time I saw this bear I'd left it with my fake suicide note on the night I abandoned my family. The reason we're in this mess."

"Right, I get that, but seriously, we're so close. This is a sign that we can still potentially save them if they're still here." Putting his hand on Phil's shoulder, DCS Terry continues, "Phil, this is not the time to give up. Come on, get your sorry ass moving." He hands Phil the bear.

"Phil, he's right," Matthew says. "We need to keep going if we're going to stand a chance."

Phil kisses the bear. "Which way?" he says.

"That's a boy. Right, keep following me, we're not far out," DCS Terry says, moving off again.

They've been battling their way through the forest for what feels like an eternity but has in actual fact only been twenty minutes or so.

"There, look! There it is," DCS Terry says with excitement.

Looking in the direction DCS Terry is pointing, Matthew sees steel fencing that appears to be fifteen feet or higher with great big points at the top. Standing behind this is a great big chapel that has overgrown vegetation surrounding it. Set back in the distance of the chapel is a building that Matthew believes to be the nunnery. This building is dark grey, and its appearance is intimidating. Accompanying this daunting atmosphere are the dark clouds, "Quick, let's go. We've not got much time– the clouds, they're becoming electric."

Matthew instantly begins to run towards the chapel. He feels sick to his stomach and his heart is beating fast, each blood-circulating pump banging against his chest. With every step he's focused only on the end result – reaching the chapel. Looking over his shoulder to Phil and DCS Terry, who are lagging behind, he shouts, "Come on. Keep up."

Reaching the back of the chapel, Matthew sees that there's no entrance through the huge steel fence surrounding the grounds. Arriving at Matthew's side, Phil and DCS Terry try to regain control of their breathing.

"We didn't plan for this, did we?" Matthew whispers.

"What are we gonna do?" Phil questions.

With his back arched and his hands on his knees, DCS Terry says, "The back entrance to the nunnery is that way." DCS Terry then points to his left, "Matthew, you need to go left, Phil, you need to stay here. I'm gonna go check out the front. Keep your radios on." DCS Terry then turns right and heads off towards the front entrance of the nunnery.

Grabbing Matthew's arm, Phil says, "Matthew, I really don't want to be here on my own. Can I come with you, please?"

Wanting to get started with searching the grounds, Matthew doesn't try to persuade Phil to stay and agrees. "Sure, just stay beside me."

"Thank you."

Abandoning the chapel, the pair then turn left and begin creeping around the fencing. Finding a slight gap, Matthew says, "Here, we need to squeeze through this. I'll go first."

He manages to get through and Phil then follows. The pair creep across the grounds. He finds a door at the back of what they believe to be the nunnery with a metal chain around it, secured by a rusty thick metal padlock. Searching around on the ground, Matthew eventually finds what looks like a huge rock. Picking this up, he feels that the texture isn't quite rock like. Looking to his hand, Matthew screams.

"What the fuck is that?" he says as he throws it in Phil's direction.

Phil dodges it and it lands on the ground. The pair look down and see it is most certainly not a rock. It's a human skull. Matthew leans over and throws up.

"Matthew, what in the God's green earth is going on here?"

Wiping his mouth, Matthew says to Phil, "Mate, please, I need you to find something that we can use to break the lock off the chain."

"Matthew, that's a skull. A human skull."

"Phil, please, just do as I've asked. We're running out of time," Matthew says as he's bent over spitting the last of the vomit onto the ground.

Frantic, Phil begins searching for a rock that isn't a human skull. Kicking the dusty dirt around, eventually Phil sees something of interest, "I've found something. Will this metal piece of the fence work?"

"Perfect. Give it here."

Passing Matthew the metal pole as he stands, Phil moves back. Matthew swings the pole against the lock, but the lock doesn't break. He swings it back once more, with greater force. This time the padlock releases and the chain drops to the floor. Matthew drops the metal pole and grabs the door handle. Looking to Phil he puts his finger to his lip and mimes, "Shh."

As he goes to open the door, DCS Terry's voice crackles through the radio. Pressing the button, Matthew says, "Terry, can you hear me?"

A crackling sound is heard again alongside DCS Terry's voice. The interference is so loud, Matthew's unable to make out what DCS Terry is saying. With a final crackle, Matthew hears, "Bodies." The radio then goes quiet.

"Terry? Terry, can you hear me?" There's no response.

"What shall we do?" Phil whispers.

Matthew ponders whether they should head to the front of what they believe to be the nunnery or continue through the back. Finally, he says, "I think we should make our way through the building this way, stay low and go find Terry at the front."

Phil nods his head. Matthew slowly pulls down the handle and opens the door. As the door creaks open a familiar pungent stench hits Matthew's nose. Putting his hand over his nose, Matthew begins to worry. What if he's too late? Making his way through the darkened corridor, Matthew grabs his phone from out of his pocket and puts on the torch. He's in what looks like the basement of the building. Seeing a staircase ahead of him, he waves at Phil to follow him.

"Right behind you, mate," Phil whispers.

Anxiously walking up the rickety staircase, Matthew finally reaches the door. He pushes it open and peers his head through the tiny gap he's created. There isn't a single person to be seen. As they make their way along the dingy dark corridor, Matthew and Phil can hear the sound of their breath leaving their bodies alongside every footstep they take. The space is outdated and does not appear to be welcoming. There are no pictures on the wall and no carpet on the floor. Just wooden floorboards throughout. On the wall are lanterns that are dimly lit. Matthew can't help but feel as if he's walking through a dungeon. Reaching the end of the corridor, Matthew sees a wooden arched door. He closes his eyes, desperately trying to regain control of his emotions and turns the door handle. As he gently pushes this open, Matthew peers through and sees yet again, there isn't a single person around. Looking to Phil, he whispers, "You okay?"

"Yeah, mate."

The pair head through the doorway and continue walking forward. Reaching yet another door, Matthew once again mines "Shh" as he pushes it open.

Peering his head in, he sees an unoccupied kitchen. There's food that has been cooked just sitting on the side. Looking down on the floor, he sees there are masses of pans, shards of glass and raw food scattered everywhere. Not only this, there's a trail of an all-too-familiar black substance. Disheartened, as he now has a great fear that they are too late, Matthew heads across the kitchen and makes his way through the door on the opposite side. Pushing it open, Matthew jumps and yelps.

"What?" Phil shouts.

"Terry, you scared the shit out of me."

"Matthew, I'm sorry. But you need to come and see this," DCS Terry says.

Looking at the expression on DCS Terry's face, Matthew realises that whatever he's about to show him is not good. They follow DCS Terry around the inside of the nunnery and eventually come to another similar looking wooden arched door. Looking to the floor, Matthew can see trails of red blood alongside the thick black substance.

"Brace yourselves," DCS Terry says as he pushes the door open.

As he walks through the doorway, Matthew's eyes are instantly drawn to the grand staircase. Looking up high, his sight travels across the landing. Matthew sees the six naked bodies swinging from a thick rope. Matthew turns his head away from the sickening image and jumps. He then stumbles into Phil and the pair land on the floor.

"Oh shit, oh shit, oh shit. Terry, who is that? Is it Eve?" Matthew frantically says with tears welling in his eyes.

"No, it's not Eve. I don't know who it is. There's one older looking female and five males. That's not the worst of it. Follow me." Putting his hands out, DCS Terry pulls Matthew and Phil up off the floor. "Mind the blood and that black crap on the floor," he says as he leads them towards the front door, which is open. "Brace yourselves."

Walking through the doorway, Matthew is mortified. There is a sea of bodies laid out across the grounds. Matthew panics as he runs down the stairway and heads to the sea of bodies. He's frantically checking each of their faces. Each person has had their eyes gouged out. Shouting, Matthew feels sick, "Eve, oh my god, Eve?"

Not making it down the steps, Phil collapses at the door.

"Terry, Phil, help me. Eve? Eve, are you here, honey? Can you hear me baby?"

Making his way over to Matthew, DCS Terry places his hand on his shoulder, "Matthew, she's not there, I've checked. None of the children are. There are just men and women. Well, men and nuns. How sad, you spend your whole life worshiping the Lord and you end up being killed by a demon. I mean, that's just unfortunate."

"Terry, oh my, what the…" Matthew says in complete shock.

"I know, I don't know what to say. We were so close." He pauses for a moment then says, "It gets worse." He turns Matthew around to face the front of the building. "Look."

Matthew looks up. Smeared across the outside of the building are the words, '**Surrender to me and I might let you live**'.

DCS Terry says, "I think you know what we need to do."

ABOUT THE AUTHOR

A.L. Frances is a thirty-two-year-old British author.

The Broken III – Control is the third book of a four-part series and marks A.L. Frances' debut in literary fiction.

Born in Wythenshawe, South Manchester, she is the product of a broken home. Her formal education was cut short before she could gain any qualifications and she became a mother to three children by the time she was just twenty years old. At twenty-one A.L. Frances suddenly finds herself cast in the role of a single parent, destined to repeat the cycle of her own difficult upbringing.

Determined to give her children a better start in life, she moved to the countryside village of Hollingworth, and eventually settled into a career in law. It was during this transition that she found herself on a journey of self-discovery. Attending multiple mindset enhancing seminars in England, America and Canada, she was exposed to the tutelage of inspirational speakers such as Bob Proctor, Tony Robbins, and Mel Robbins among others. A.L. Frances was eventually introduced to Peggy McColl, a New York Times Best Selling Author. Standing on the stage, Peggy said the words that would inspire her into action. Peggy said, "Everyone has a book in them." as she pointed into the crowd. It was at this point that A.L. Frances fell in love with the idea of writing her own book and telling her own story; one that would address one of her biggest fears: the vulnerabilities of broken homes.

At the age of twenty-nine, A.L. Frances decided it was time to start the next chapter of her life.

What follows is the start of her journey…